SAY A LITTLE MANTRA FOR ME

SAY A LITTLE MANTRA FOR ME

FOR ME

Yvonne Burgess

PENGUIN BOOKS

PENGUIN BOOKS

Published by the Penguin Group
Penguin Books Ltd, 80 Strand, London WC2R 0RL, England
Penguin Group (USA) Inc, 375 Hudson Street, New York, New York 10014,
USA
Penguin Group (Canada), 90 Eglinton Avenue East, Suite 700, Toronto,
Ontario, Canada M4P 2Y3 (a division of Pearson Penguin Canada Inc)
Penguin Ireland, 25 St Stephen's Green, Dublin 2, Ireland (a division of
Penguin Books Ltd)
Penguin Group (Australia), 250 Camberwell Road, Camberwell, Victoria 3124,
Australia (a division of Pearson Australia Group Pty Ltd)
Penguin Books India Pvt Ltd, 11 Community Centre, Panchsheel Park, New
Delhi – 110 017, India
Penguin Group (NZ), Cnr Rosedale and Airborne Roads, Albany, Auckland
1310, New Zealand (a division of Pearson New Zealand Ltd)
Penguin Books (South Africa) (Pty) Ltd, 24 Sturdee Avenue, Rosebank,
Johannesburg 2196, South Africa

Penguin Books (South Africa) (Pty) Ltd, Registered Offices:
24 Sturdee Avenue, Rosebank, Johannesburg 2196, South Africa

www.penguinbooks.co.za

First published by Ravan Press (Pty) Ltd in 1979
This edition published by Penguin Books (South Africa) (Pty) Ltd 2006

Copyright © Yvonne Burgess 1979

ISBN 0 143 02470 1

Typeset by CJH in 10/12.5 pt Palatino
Cover design: African Icons
Cover image: GalloImages/gettyimages.com
Printed and bound by Interpak Books, Pietermaritzburg

Vern

'Cities can dent your dharma,' I'd told her. 'And crowds with indifferent eyes.'

But it didn't look as though she'd understood, or even wanted to. So how to go on, about trying to keep one's thongs on the noble eightfold path when right desire which is no desire hardens into wrong desire and abstinence which is right conduct becomes the sort of conduct that shouldn't be conducted at all, especially out there, in among the sand dunes ...

Because that was how it was getting with Girlie and me.

I was giving out all the right words but words don't control a man's destiny, only actions, and at the rate I was acting, my current life in conflagration, the last dewdrop would be swallowed up by the shining sea long before I ever got near nirvana; but when I finally told her I'd got to split, her laughter slipped and she looked suddenly blank and blue.

I talked ethics and discipline; said I was doing both of us a favour, she didn't want to go on living, did she, coming back for ever and ever, never merging with universal life?

She said: 'Uh, nooo ...'

'Right on,' I said, because I'd explained it all to her, like acquiring merit in successive chains of lives and the four noble truths.

That was when she mumbled the 'maybe, perhaps you're right' bit, and said: 'Don't go ...'

Vibes like those coming from her just then almost made me say fag the noble truths and the path and the law of karma and everything else, even nirvana, but that would have set me back by about a thousand lives, so I tried again:

'Existence is unhappy only for as long as desire is selfish. We've all got to lose selfish desire. Meditate. Achieve yama and desire becomes extinct.'

'Surely,' she said, but the way she was looking at me unnerved me, so that I nearly practised right speech then, truthful and plain and so painful that I'd even tried to hide it from myself, about the angst that built up until it had me physically, by the legs, palms, the soles of my feet, like a million grubs just under the skin, so real that I had to keep looking, expecting to see them burrowing there. They spoilt me for sleeping and eating and thinking. I'd blow my mind if I didn't split.

But imaginary bugs are personal things so I got a hold of myself before going on:

'The sixth step is the answer. Right effort. Always pressing on along the eightfold path and after a mile or two you begin to be able to breathe again ...'

That was interpreting it rather literally, I knew, but it had always worked before, getting out there among the willows and the pines and the fever trees. I'd always felt better, the grubs always quietened down as soon as I saw the hornbills and the rollers and the sky opening up ahead of me; when I could swing out, stretching my knees, like wearing seven-league sandals, to where everything was like it had always been, where there was no sweat, no grubby fingerprints, and no hacking cough in the night. I thought she was beginning to understand. At least it looked as though she was trying, so I said:

'There'll be another summer,' not sure whether I meant it myself, because all I could think of just then was the road and the angst that would soon be sweating itself out of me, leaving me free, like my actions were my own, like I was controlling my destiny, all set on the noble eightfold path.

'Another summer,' she said. 'Go well then. And say a little mantra for me.'

Part One

1

Mother

'Just listen to this: "Depression, claustrophobia, disturbed sleep, loss of appetite, fits of temper, bouts of weeping".'

I waited for Gran to recognise at least some of the symptoms. But Gran doesn't like recognising symptoms; she prefers discovering them. 'They call it flat neurosis,' I told her. 'It says here if people don't have space, an area to themselves, they get flat neurosis.'

'Oh,' Gran said. 'I read that. And I can tell you it's arrant nonsense. *And* I can tell you why.'

Sometimes I can't help it, my curiosity gets the better of me, so I had to ask: 'Oh, why?' although that meant giving Gran the satisfaction.

'Stands to reason, doesn't it?' Gran said. 'If it wasn't nonsense I'd be the one to catch it, wouldn't I? I'm the one who's shut up in a flat all the time. But I haven't got it, and I can tell you why.'

I hated to give Gran the satisfaction twice in one evening, but I had to ask: 'Oh, why?' again, because after all these years Gran's mentality still fascinates me.

She leaned forward like she always does when she's about to give Girlie or me one of her 'nuggets' that Girlie used to call 'nuts' when she was younger.

'Because I'm prepared to put up with it,' Gran said. 'That's what life is all about. Putting up with things. And if *you've* got anything, Iris, it's from dieting, not from a flat. Because the human body is like a machine, any mechanic will tell you that, and if it doesn't get fuel it's going to get depressed and disturbed sleep and fits of temper and all the rest of it. Stands to reason.'

There was never any point in arguing with Gran. If she

was ever actually proved wrong she'd get out of it by saying she knew it all along, only she didn't like to say so. Like that time she'd diagnosed asthma for Mrs McKechnie's husband and plastered his chest with all sorts of poultices and when he finally died of cirrhosis, she said she'd known it all along but hadn't liked to say so on account of cirrhosis not being such a terribly respectable thing to die of.

I took up the newspaper again and I thought, it's all right for Gran. She had the whole place to herself for most of the day while I had my head stuck between the filing cabinet and the air conditioner in that cupboard of an office, and when we were all at home there was nowhere to go except the bathroom, if you wanted some privacy, and you weren't left in there in peace for very long either, not with Gran around.

Depression and claustrophobia. I knew all about it. Feeling shut up and panicky and wanting to claw the walls. Disturbed sleep too, although I'd had that for years; long before we moved into the flat I'd be lying awake smoking all night wondering how it was all going to end, and even sometimes whether I should end it.

Fits of temper and weeping. I knew all about it, never mind what Gran said. Because what did it matter what you called it?

Girlie must have been feeling it too. She was avoiding me. She didn't say anything but she was looking depressed, and she wasn't eating much. Maybe it was still in the early stages, maybe any day now she'd get the rest, the claustrophobia and the temper and the weeping. I wouldn't be able to stand that. Not two of us, with Gran adding her ha'pennyworth.

It hadn't been too bad while Girlie was still at school, but she was growing up, developing her own tastes. She'd decorated her corner of our room with posters and peace signs and pop stars at first and that was bad enough even when you got used to it, all the blank faces and long lank hair and a ruby stuck in a navel, but lately she'd been sticking up Indians with burning eyes and long lank beards and I felt embarrassed getting undressed at night.

Gurus, she called them. It didn't sound decent, and I said, you'd better not let Gran hear *that*.

And then she spent most of her time sitting cross-legged reciting some weird gibberish. She said they were mantras, to aid in concentration and I told her she'd better not let Gran know about it or *she'd* have something to say.

Girlie needed a room of her own, and it wasn't right, but I couldn't help thinking: since Gran obviously wasn't going to pass on in the near future, couldn't I talk her into a Home? Then again, when Girlie had been at it for ages, muttering her mantras and miles away, I'd think, no, it's better to have her right here in the room with me, where I can keep an eye on her.

I didn't know what to do. I just sat there, thinking around and around in the same old circle and it wasn't until Gran got up that I realised that I hadn't read a single line of that newspaper in about half an hour.

Gran

'What was in that parcel you brought home then?' I asked Iris. 'A new dress?' I could see she wasn't reading. She was ruminating again, and chewing her cuticles.

'Mind if I have a look?' I asked, just to take her out of herself. She said 'um' or maybe 'uh-um', but she went to get it anyway.

Quite pretty from the point of view of colour, I thought, but apart from that it'd got nothing to it. I pulled a little thread sticking out of a button and the whole thing came off just like that. I could see the pockets were false too and I wasn't surprised. They've always got to have something false on these days. It's the way the world is going.

'What'd you do that for?' Iris asks me as if I'd done something.

'I didn't do anything,' I told her. 'It's the machines they use these days. There's only one way to sew on a button and that's by hand, in and out and through and through, not like they do it today, all you've got to do is pull one thread and the whole dress falls apart.'

'Well don't pull any more for God's sake,' she says and grabs the dress out of my hands. But not before I'd had a chance to look inside. Not one of the seams overcast properly, just that loose zigzagging they do these days, and the hem too.

'You've just got to pull one thread,' I warned her, 'and the whole thing is going to unravel on your back. You've just got to be sitting next to someone on the bus and ...'

'All right Gran for God's sake,' Iris says.

I was beginning to think Iris could do with a tonic, the way she was chewing at her fingers and blaspheming. She's never heard me blaspheming.

Girlie wandered in just then and that was another thing. You never see that gel in a nice little frock these days.

'Why don't we see you in a nice little frock these days?' I asked her.

'No one wears frocks any more Gran,' she says to me.

'I do,' I told her. 'Been wearing them for years.'

The same ones too. Trouble is they're so well made I'll have to go on wearing them. Maybe that's why they make them like that these days, so's they'll fall apart the first little thread you pull. No wonder Iris has to have a wardrobe full. I never had a wardrobe full in my life, and that put me in mind of my trousseau that I wore for ten years. All hand sewn it was. I must have started it when I was around Girlie's age, and that put me in mind of Girlie again.

'What's Girlie doing about her bottom drawer?' I asked Iris.

'Her what?' Iris asks.

'Her trousseau,' I said, 'for when she gets married. You're not about to let your only daughter be married in jeans, Iris?'

A bit sarcastic, perhaps, but it provoked me, the way they pretended never to understand anything I said.

'With all the sacrifices we're making,' Iris snaps at me, 'Girlie'd better get her degree first.'

'She'll not want to wait until the last minute,' I warned Iris. 'I remember when I was around her age ...'

'All right!' Iris cuts me off pretty sharp, and I could see that she didn't want to think about Girlie's bottom drawer, at least not while she was still hoping she'd have one of her own to think about. Iris never could make the best of things.

'Well, you can just tell that gel,' I said, 'that she's not got to worry about her bottom drawer as long as her old Gran can sew on a button or two so's they'll stick, not that her eyes are what they used to be, but ...'

At that Iris ups and bounces out. 'I'll make some tea,' she says.

I picked at the dress again, keeping an ear on Iris because she was nipping a bit too much lately and I was beginning to suspect that she'd got something hidden in the kitchen, the way she was always bouncing up to make tea whenever I was in the middle of saying something. But she was filling the kettle all right. She'd never put that much water in her gin.

Girlie

I could hear Mother banging and clattering about in the kitchen making tea, but I tried to shut out the noise, sitting quietly under the Maharishi, like Vern had been sitting the first time I saw him, only he'd been outside the life-saver's hut, sifted over with sand like he'd been there for centuries. He was as brown as an Indian and I thought wow! what's an Indian in a trance doing on our beach?

But he wasn't an Indian and he wasn't in a trance. His eyes were open and he was looking at me so I had to say something.

'What are you doing?' I asked.

'Meditating,' he said.

'Wow,' I said. 'What for?'

'Meditation,' he told me, 'leads to right action.' It was the way he said it that grabbed me.

'Can I do it too?' I asked.

And that was how it started, Vern and me meditating, focusing on the small point of stillness that he said was inside all of us, feeling the heat of the sun trapped in the dunes long after the sky had turned purple.

It led to action all right and it must have been the right action because it was so natural. Like Vern said, you wouldn't try to change the drift of a cloud or the fall of water. But if you let those things be which were natural and rode with them there'd never be any sweat.

'Dare the hurricane,' he said, 'and it'll blow you away.'

And it wasn't until summer had gone, leaving the beach bleak and windy and empty with little drifts of sand piling up against the tufts of dry grass that there was any sweat. Because that was when Vern said it was getting to be time for him to go.

'Go where?' I asked him.

'Follow the stars,' he said, 'to the North where they hang like lanterns over the bushveld, or maybe even Kathmandu.'

'But why?' I asked.

'Because I've never been there,' he said.

'I mean, why go?'

'Because action must alternate with repose,' he said, 'like speech with silence.'

I wanted to say it, but I thought, no.

'Look,' Vern said, 'the beach scene is over. Until next summer anyway. If I stay here what will I do? Where will I go? Into the city where all that concrete and clamour jams my vibes and jangles my dharma?'

I said it then, just that once: 'Don't go.' And for the first time since I'd known him he lost that sleepy stoned look of his, and I was sorry I'd said it, because if he stayed it'd got to be because he wanted to.

Maybe he wanted to, but he didn't stay. He'd earned enough bread for a while, enough to split, to where the stars were near and bright, he'd said, until maybe next summer ...

I tried to locate my inner point of stillness but I couldn't find it because I couldn't empty my mind. I kept hearing Mother in the kitchen and even seeing her, lunging at everything, the kettle, the cups and the caddy which must have slipped because there was a loud tinny clang and Gran yelled: 'Save the pieces!'

I looked for an object to concentrate on. There was the crumpled mound of brown paper on Mother's bed that looked like a camel and a magazine called *Love and Your Life*. I fixed on the *Love* because that was the first of the four virtuous acts, but then the kettle began to wheeze and gargle like it was being throttled so I tried to get on to resignation but my toes started to tingle and I knew I was going to get pins and needles and that would be the end of it.

It was. Maybe you had to have stars that were near and bright before you could begin to feel part of the universal order. And I thought, maybe that's what they were trying to say, those psychologists Mother was telling Gran about. Maybe that was what flat neurosis really was: being literally, physically, boxed off from the universal order.

Because we couldn't even *see* the stars; at least not without hanging out of a window and ricking our necks. And even then all we saw most nights was smoke from the power station.

2

Gran

I lay awake a long while that night, thinking, and I thought: if anyone was going to catch anything from living in a flat it should be Esmé McKechnie, squashed in like that with her son and daughter-in-law and two small children, in the lounge/dinette with her bed hard up against the sideboard next to last Christmas's Christmas cake, or the year before's, the way it was mouldering away.

But Esmé hasn't got anything that I can see. It's like water off a duck's back to her which just goes to show it's those who've had a lot to put up with that can always put up with a little bit extra. Because Esmé hasn't had an easy time of it, not with old Mac drinking like a fish and suffering from it, although she should have expected that, marrying an Irishman or whatever he was, because they all drink like fish. Rhodesians too, as she's always telling me in bits and pieces on the stairs because she won't talk in front of Nova, who isn't turning out to be good enough for Patrick, just like she warned him right after the wedding.

She's had a hard life all right, has Esmé. In the end old Mac even used to wet the bed.

'And you never thought of divorcing him?' I asked her once, before she told me they were Catholic, but I'm broad-minded and I still took him the poultices round when he got bad.

At least Mac always talked straight, Esmé said, like the time she had her operation, her 'sterectomy, and he stood at the bottom of the bed and told her now she wasn't fish nor fowl, and he had his moments too, playing the guitar for her and singing Mountains of Mourne. He never squinted and hinted – like Nova did, unless she and Patrick wanted to go out, and then it was, Mom have you got enough cigarettes and Mom

12

make yourself some tea, but the other day when Esmé fried herself a sausage, she said she was that hungry, Nova went sniffing around the fridge to see if she'd taken anything else.

No, Esmé has a lot to put up with and she isn't all that healthy either with the trouble her glands have been giving her ever since the operation. And her stomach has dropped too, she says, because there's nothing underneath to hold it up any more.

Compared with Esmé, I thought, Iris had got nothing to chew her cuticles about. But there she was, fretting and fussing and reading the bleeding hearts when she thought I wasn't looking, which wasn't often, and won't be for as long as I can help it.

Mother

I was reading them secretly, like you have to do everything that matters in this flat, and I thought, I don't compare too badly. I had a good, cheap, pre-war flat with a pegged rent, a good steady job and if I took some trouble I could look quite attractive. I wouldn't make all sorts of stipulations about height, weight, finances, church-going, encumbrances or even a car, although that would be nice, with a view to weekend outings. I wouldn't make any stipulations at all, and I could honestly say I was home-loving – I hadn't had much chance to be anything else. At least I could cook. I might have liked gardening too, if I'd had a garden, and I'm sure I could be a good mixer, if I had someone to mix with.

The only thing was the encumbrances. The most promising-sounding of them always drew the line at encumbrances.

No encumbrances please.

I'd have to be honest, lay it all on the table: *Own flat, job, hazel eyes, divorced, thirty-nine, home-loving, fond of cooking, gardening, weekend outings, sincere, honest and encumbered with elderly mother and teenage daughter.* And if I wanted to be really honest, *irritating elderly mother and obstinate teenage daughter.*

Who'd reply to that? There'd be no point in stopping at *weekend outings, expenses shared.* They were all looking for someone, whether they said so or not, *with a view to.*

And of course I also had a view to. Otherwise why say *no chancers, please*?

I knew it wasn't nice, but I couldn't help thinking, Gran's got to go some time and Girlie will get married and then where will I be? So I went on reading them.

I liked the sound of *Executive* who had a *happy and affectionate nature* and offered *outings, club and dance dates.* I could hardly remember when I had last gone dancing. *Viking* was *tall, good-looking, active,* had a good position and *considerable assets.* All he wanted was someone who *still believed in love.* My own belief in love had had some of the stuffing knocked out of it, but I was still prepared to be convinced, God knew. Especially by someone like *Mister X* who was *kind, intelligent and hearty* and liked *elegant living.*

I nearly answered that one, but I couldn't see Gran and Girlie fitting into elegant living, even supposing he had nothing against encumbrances, Gran in her grey aprons and slippers and Girlie with the edges of her jeans frayed, and not only frayed, but deliberately frayed.

Capricorn sounded more hopeful: *secure, six foot, 175 pounds* and *welcomes children.* Not that Girlie was a child, exactly. And could *welcomes children* be stretched to include Gran?

Those were the best ones. Some of the others sounded a bit off. A drag, as Girlie would have said. Like *Stranger on the Shore* who adored Science but hated *frigidity, irrationality and apartheid,* or *Cupid* who was in his seventies and was looking for a *bundle of mischief. Dreamer* was sure his *soul-mate is in orbit* but didn't say what he expected of her on splash-down, and *Braaivleis* was feeling, like me, *the chill of winter and also of life.* Some of the proposed *weekend outings* depended on the *sincere, honest lady* having a car, which I didn't have, but all of them insisted on *a sense of humour.*

I had one, I was sure, only it was wearing a bit thin. Nothing, I considered, could be less conducive to good humour than sitting around the flat with Gran and Girlie all the time. What I needed, if my sense of humour was ever going to revive, was a few weekend outings, club dates and dances, all of them definitely *with a view to.*

So I began to write. To *Executive, Viking* and *Walk With Me.* They didn't reply. I'd mentioned Gran and Girlie as humorously as I could, but they didn't answer.

They would have had lots of replies, I told myself, from younger, unencumbered ladies. Competition was bound to be keen, and maybe I hadn't managed to make Girlie and Gran sound funny enough.

After that I decided to draft my own advert. I must have done about fifty of them, with different pseudonyms, but in the end I decided on, quite simply, *Hazel Eyes* and I kept it short: age, height, job, flat, home-loving, sincere, sense of humour and teenage daughter. I would have said *honest* as well if I'd been able to mention Gran. But I couldn't, not immediately. If anyone did reply, though, I would mention her – *aged mother* – in the very first letter. Teenage daughters could be left to the imagination, after all. Teenage daughters are bound to get married. But I didn't feel right about leaving Gran's inevitable passing on to the imagination. At least, not in an advert.

Girlie

I went into one crazy calculation after another in my head, trying to tie up dates with incidents and actions, hoping that it was juggling with all those figures that was making me nauseous, that somehow I had made a stupid mistake, but counting up to twenty-eight isn't all that difficult so I knew I hadn't made a mistake and that made the nausea worse.

I got a big textbook on gynaecology out of the library and put a brown paper cover on it. Even then I hardly dared to open it except in the jazz which was fortunate because when I read that I was carrying an embryo shaped like a pear, with eyes and ears starting to form on it, with a tube for a heart, something that was going to be a tongue and 'limb buds', it sounded so awful and deformed, like a Thalidomide baby, that I had to get sick in the basin with the tap running so no one would hear. If I had known how, I would have got rid of that awful pear with its tube and buds right then but I didn't, so I washed my face and sat down to think about Vern which always helped when I got hassled.

You had to let those things be which were natural.

He hadn't put it quite like that, of course. He'd explained about the oneness of everything, the oneness of time and eternity, that he called samsara and nirvana.

I couldn't see how any of that was going to help me now, except that in a way time, or the next seven or so months of it, was going to be an eternity all right.

That wasn't the way he'd meant it, and it wasn't going to grab Mother and Gran much, that idea, not as an explanation, anyway, let alone an excuse. And the other, more ordinary explanation, about how, when once we'd held hands, everything just went on from there, like the drift of a cloud or the fall of water, like we couldn't have stopped it any more than dare a hurricane, wouldn't grab them either, so I thought I wouldn't explain, I'd just have to let it be, at least for the time being.

Gran

'Mind what you say in front of Girlie, Gran,' Iris says to me. 'Don't talk about bottom drawers and things like that, giving her ideas. She's at an awkward age.'

Awkward age. Everyone's at an awkward age. I'm at an awkward age. The papers are full of the problems of old age. Every age has its problems. But that's life, isn't it? That's the way we're tested.

'Don't you feel it?' I was asking Esmé McKechnie on the stairs just the other day. 'The problems of old age?'

But all she can think about these days is the problems of her grandson who's a problem child.

We never had them, and if we did they were spoilt brats, but today they're problem children, which comes to the same thing only it sounds nicer, I suppose.

'Every family's got its cross,' I told Esmé to make her feel better, 'maybe he is eleven years and only going into Standard 2. But he'll come on. You'll see. They all come on.'

The trouble is that Esmé's a Catholic so she has to go to the priest who never had any children so what does he know about it, like that time young Patrick did his business on a piece of newspaper and covered it over with a whole wad of toilet paper and then blocked up the lav with it.

'And what did the priest say about that?' I asked her. 'Did he say to give him a good leathering and make him clean up his own mess?'

'Oh no,' Esmé says. 'He's a problem child. He's got a complex.'

I couldn't see what a complex had to do with doing his business on a piece of newspaper.

'And what did the priest say?'

'He told Nova to take him to the Child Guidance.'

'And what did *they* say?' I asked.

'They said he's a problem child,' she says, as if she didn't know that already, so what did she have to go there for in the first place? And she's poorly herself, Esmé. But now Patrick's going to a boarding school.

'It's the best thing for a boy like that,' she says.

So now he'll be blocking up the boarding school toilets and they won't stand for that.

'He'd better not block the boarding school toilets,' I said to her. 'They won't stand for that, problem child or no problem child.'

And that's a fact. Get a good leathering from the headmaster or the teachers, I should think. Brothers, they call them. Brothers and Sisters and Fathers and Bishops and Popes. Catholics. And too many children between the lot of them, I should think, with Nova expecting again and Esmé already squashed up against the Christmas cake. No wonder they have problem children.

We never had any problem with Girlie. I know it's not true what they say about the convents, but if the Brothers and the Fathers are so busy with the Sisters they might not have time to give the kids a good leathering. Even Esmé, and she's one of them herself, only got shown into a little waiting room, she says, so if they've got nothing to hide what's all the mystery for, I'd like to know.

But he'll keep them busy, all right, Master Patrick McKechnie Jnr. Only they'll make him clean up his own mess and keep him in the chapel reciting Hail Marys, for all the good that will do him.

Only I didn't like to say so to Esmé, the poor woman, when he is her own grandchild; we've got to have some charity in this wicked world, and at least they don't believe in abortions.

3

Mother

Gin and tonic tastes just like bile, I decided. Like wormwood and gall. And the telephone never rang.

'When did the phone last ring?' I asked Gran.

'If you're hinting about the rental,' she said, 'we've got to have a phone with me alone here most of the day. What if someone breaks in? I could have a stroke.'

'I was only trying to remember when it last rang,' I said.

And then I thought, maybe I could ring someone. But who? There was only Phoebe, and she gave up on everything years ago. Especially herself. The last time I saw her she looked like an over-inflated rubber seahorse with a widow's peak and she breathed loudly through her nose all the time. Short-sighted too, although she can't help that.

In any case she never answers her phone any more, and if she does she just breathes into it and then puts it down again. Says hippies have been bothering her. I wished someone would bother me.

It wouldn't do any good, phoning Phoebe. She was worse off than I was. I'd get no comfort or cheer from her. Living all alone like that and giving up hope has made her go queer. I probably shouldn't have friends like Phoebe.

And then I thought, to hell with Gran, and had another gin, with orange juice so it wouldn't taste so much like bile.

I needed a holiday. Only the last time I went away, to Johannesburg, it was terrible. Terribly lonely. I walked the streets just to get out of that hotel room, and I walked fast, pretending I had somewhere to go, or at least that where I was going was somewhere more exciting than a matinée. And when I'd seen every film in town I saw an advert for a Friendship Club in the paper. It cost me two rand to get in and

I got a glass of cheap wine and a number pairing me off with a little round man of about fifty who acted as though he couldn't believe I was divorced, although what else would I be doing there, I wondered. He was divorced too, he said, and he said, wait until they put the lights out and I'll tell you why.

I didn't know they were going to put the lights out, I thought it was just a Friendship Club, but they did and he started kissing and pawing me while I tried to hang on to my wine which was slopping all over the place.

'I'll tell you,' he said, when he had to stop for breath. 'My ex-wife was a selfish bitch, she'd have hers and then she'd go limp and I'd have to poke, poke, like into the ashes of a dead fire. It soured me, her going limp like that. How about you?' and he started kissing and pawing me again. I said I was the same, even worse, and I got out of there fast because cold, calculated sex isn't my bag, as Girlie would put it.

No, my bag, I thought, because gin always makes me morbid, is just getting to be old, drying up and blowing away.

I got up, but when I saw Gran watching the level of the gin bottle through the holes in the cloth she was crocheting for Girlie's bottom drawer, I sat down again.

Girlie

You read about people feeling like a part of them is missing, you see them in films, and it does feel like that, like you've had something amputated, like you're minus something really vital.

It had always been a bit of a drag from time to time, depending on Mother and Gran, like now, with Mother trying to mesmerise the phone into ringing or Gran into not noticing that she's pouring another gin, and Gran acting as if Mrs McKechnie's grandson was a problem child just to spite her and insinuating that being a Catholic had something to do with it. It was bad enough, but when I thought of how they were going to be when they found out about me, that's when I really began to feel as if my nervous system had blown a fuse or some of the oxygen was missing out of the air.

They'd never let things be and ride them out. Things were always riding them out, even before they happened, like burglars breaking in or having a stroke or the phone ringing or not ringing.

I just had to prepare them a little bit for what *was* going to happen, but it was difficult because I was still trying to prepare myself. Not that there was all that much time for preparation either, and I kept thinking that if I didn't start in on them soon there was going to be no time at all. So, I got my own thoughts more or less straight on the necessary levels of attainment and started in. Mother wasn't ready for terms like pratyahara or dharana, let alone Gran who quite often got stuck on ordinary English words, so I started in as simply as I could:

'There's no percentage in being attached to the senses, is there? I mean, too attached?' I asked them.

They looked at me, waiting for me to carry on, I suppose, and make whatever point I was making; only that *was* the point and if they didn't get it it was going to be difficult to explain, except in the way I wanted them to understand it, which was that we should free our souls to get above purely physical considerations, like having a baby, but of course I couldn't say that.

'What I mean is,' I tried again, 'one has to see the thing as a whole, hasn't one?'

Mother, was getting suspicious like she always does when she thinks I'm trying to pull my education on her.

'What thing?' she said.

I couldn't tell her *that* yet, not before she was prepared, so I said:

'Well, everything, I suppose.'

Gran was staring at me undecided, waiting to see which way Mother was going to jump so that she could jump the other way, so when Mother said:

'*Please* don't talk rubbish, Girlie, I've had a hard day,' Gran said: 'Now Iris, that's exactly what the newspapers are always on about, we don't *listen* to our young people, so no wonder there's this terrible gap these days.'

'You just tell your Gran, my gel,' she said to me. 'Gran's interested in all your little ideas,' and she put her crochet hook down and folded her hands and leaned forward with that patient, inviting look that always drove Mother wild and chased every single idea I ever did have clean out of my head.

'Gran's listening, dear,' she said, even more patient and inviting, hoping to get Mother wilder, and I would have dropped it, except that I simply *had* to prepare them for their own good, so I said:

'It's not a *little* idea, Gran, it's been accepted for nearly two and a half thousand years.'

'What idea was that?' Mother asked, just in case there was something to it and then she could pretend she hadn't heard the first time, or Gran would be one up on her.

They played that sort of game all the time and I would have left them to it if it hadn't been so important to get them thinking along the right lines before I dropped my real bomb. So I told them again:

'It's important to free the mind so that old things, like, well, things that can happen to the body, you know, don't throw you, and it's all just a part of the universal order so you don't have to get all hassled about it, you know?'

Mother and Gran looked at each other then like they always do when there's something they don't understand and they feel they'd better face it together, especially when it's something they don't understand about *me*.

'The body?' Mother asked.

'Can't be anything serious, Iris,' Gran said. 'Her eyes are quite clear.'

'It's not her eyes I'm worried about,' Mother said, 'it's her

22

head.'

They didn't even notice when I got up and walked out, they were so hard at it, Mother moaning that if I *was* sick, how much was the doctor going to cost, and Gran wondering about brain fever because she's never thought book work and concentration were meant for a girl and so on and on and so depressing that I felt exactly as I had when I watched Vern walking away along the beach, with the last of the bathers gone and the life-saver's hut locked and the brightness fading steadily from the sun.

I had to get my mind off that but the only other thing I could think about was the baby which wasn't even a baby yet but only a pear with eyes and limb buds, so I made myself stop thinking and sat up straight with my legs folded and repeated 'Om, om, om', which is the shortest and easiest mantra to remember but I couldn't concentrate so I tried to fix on an image instead. The lotus is the best and most sacred but the way Vern had drawn it in the sand for me it looked like the picture on a tin of bamboo shoots which wasn't very sacred at all and you only had to strip off a few layers and you were right back to the pear.

4

Gran

I'll say this for Iris; she's never yet said outright 'I want you to go into a Home.' But whenever there's something in the papers about how nice it is for the old folks she reads it out to me, as if I couldn't read it for myself. Like this evening when she said to me:

'There's this nice new Home for old folks opened up,' she says. 'They're going to cultivate life-enriching physical and mental activities for the residents.'

'Oh,' I said, as if I was interested. 'And how are they going to set about doing that?'

'Well,' she says, 'there will be recreational, cultural, religious and social meetings.'

'I was never one for meetings,' I told her straight.

'And braai facilities,' she says.

'You've got to have false teeth that really fit for that,' I told her.

'And croquet,' she says, 'and jukskei.'

That made me laugh. The best laugh I'd had in years. 'Jukskei,' I said. 'I can just see myself. Can't you just see me playing jukskei?'

Even Iris couldn't see it. 'Well, indoor games then,' she says. 'And a library, and art and craft classes.'

'That's better,' I said. 'But you know, there's only one thing wrong with old people's Homes.'

'Oh, and what's that?' she asks, looking relieved that it's only one thing.

'They're full of old people,' I said. 'I was reading about a man who went to prison rather than stay in an old people's Home. He said too many people die there. Isn't that downright depressing? You're just getting to know someone, playing croquet or indoor games with them and the next thing you know they've popped off. Who feels like playing croquet when the people you're playing with are popping off like balloons around you all the time?'

'I don't think it can be as bad as that,' Iris says. 'And they've even got a shopping centre.'

'So have I,' I reminded her, 'just around the corner. And no one here is going to pop off. Except me. I'm the only one that's likely to pop off around here.'

'Oh, Mother,' Iris says.

I know she doesn't like that. It suits her to pretend that I'm not going to pop off, so I have to remind her from time to time.

'But before I pop off,' I told her, 'there are a few things to be done around here.'

'About what?' Iris asks, getting a bit wary.

'About Girlie,' I told her. 'Have you noticed how peaked she's looking lately? Peaked and pale, with her eyes bagging, at her age?'

'She's at an awkward age,' Iris tells me again. 'I think she had a crush on some boy, that long-haired life-saver, I think, but she'll get over it. It's only natural.'

'Well, a tonic won't do her any harm,' I said. 'She's supposed to be washing her hands all the time but I think her tummy's upset, I can hear it, tap running and all that flushing. She's got no energy, that gel, sitting cross-legged on her bed all the time. I think she's outgrowing her strength, so I'll just mix her up a bit of my tonic, get her back on her feet and she'll stop brooding about that crush in no time.'

'If it's *that* tonic,' Iris says, 'you'd better leave out the rum. She's only turned eighteen.'

'And what sort of a tonic will it be without the rum?' I asked her.

Iris has got no idea of these things. Drinking gin and tonic all the time that isn't a tonic at all, like she does, and far too much of it lately, if you ask me, like she's a bit nervous or

25

something, a bit of a real tonic wouldn't do her any harm either, I thought.

So I mixed up a bit extra, six eggs covered with lemon juice, shells and all, to get the goodness out of the chicken scratchings, and when they had gone soft I put them through a sieve and added half a bottle of rum and a jar of honey. A tablespoonful night and morning would see them both right. It'd calm Iris down and buck Girlie up.

And come to think of it, it wouldn't do me any harm either, so I put in three more eggs which meant we'd have to make do with only cereal for breakfast for a week or so, but then you can't have everything.

Mother

'There's a letter for you,' Gran said as soon as I got home. 'From a man.'

'How do you know it's from a man?' I asked. Gran often amazes me.

'It's a man's handwriting,' she said. 'All thick and bold.'

My stomach suddenly felt hollow and my heart gave a little flutter. Somehow I hadn't thought that anyone would reply. 'Where is it then?' I asked.

'Next to the marmalade,' she said.

I put my handbag down and stood humming a while so as not to appear too eager.

'Aren't you going to open it?' Gran asked.

It began to annoy me, the way she was hovering around. 'When I'm good and ready,' I said.

That must have annoyed her.

'I know all about it, you know,' she said.

'What do you know about it, for God's sake,' I asked, because I didn't know anything about it myself, yet. 'What is there to know?'

Gran sighed one of her put-upon sighs. 'Well, it can't be a letter from a lawyer,' she said, 'because you can't be coming into any money or anything, so it must be something else and since you've been reading these bleeding hearts for months on end now and I wasn't born yesterday, I can put two and two together, can't I?'

I poured a gin to distract her but for once it didn't work.

'And it isn't a matter of what there is to know,' she went on, 'it's a matter of what there *will* be to know that's more to the point. Because you're bound to be burning your fingers, Iris, playing with fire, writing to strange men like that. There's bound to be something wrong with men who've got to advertise themselves in the papers like this week's snip. They'll be irregular, you mark my words.'

'Irregular?' I thought maybe she meant they'd be queer.

'Like jerseys put out on special offer,' she said.

'Oh,' I said, feeling a bit confused, but maybe that was from the gin which I had gulped rather too quickly, to calm myself. 'Well, perhaps I'd better go and see,' I said, 'although where jerseys come into it ...'

I wiped the marmalade off the envelope and went through to the bedroom but Girlie was there, sitting cross-legged on the floor. Gran was right. She did have bags under her eyes.

'Are you taking Gran's tonic?' I asked her.

She shook her head and turned a bit pale.

'You should be out in the fresh air more often,' I told her. 'Get a bit of sun. And just remember that tonic is damned expensive, all that rum and nine whole eggs to get the chicken scratchings, Gran tells me ...'

Girlie went even paler, clapped her hand to her mouth and ran to the bathroom. I thought, Gran's right. Her tummy must be upset. I'd have to take her to Dr Shaw if it didn't clear up soon, but now at last, and in private, I could read the letter.

I skipped the preliminary politenesses and went straight on to the body which I read once and then again, more slowly, because I thought someone must be having me on:

Anita, my ex-wife, was so ugly that it was a sort of perfection. She reminded me of that old Mutt and Jeff joke: is that your nose or are you eating a banana? I hope you haven't got that sort of a nose. I've got a thing about noses, now, after all those years of it, because it was always getting in the way. She couldn't help it but I couldn't help feeling the way I did either, so if you haven't got a good nose, a really perfect, beautiful nose, it won't be any good for us, I'm sorry ...

Girlie came back just then so I had to go to the bathroom, and I thought, in spite of the slight state of shock I was in, that it was like musical chairs in that flat, like Darby and Joan. And I had to admit that Gran was right. There was something irregular about that letter.

I sat down on the toilet and thought about my nose and his ex-wife's nose for a bit and then I got up to look in the mirror.

My nose wasn't *too* bad, I thought, but it wasn't perfect either. The nostrils were always flaring like an old horse that had been pushed too far. And I couldn't draw them in without pulling the rest of my face out of shape.

Tension, I suppose, tension and the general strain of having Girlie at an awkward age with a tummy upset, and Gran who thought she was the Great Physician and Sherlock Holmes rolled into one with her concoctions and putting two and two together.

I remembered reading about sleeping with a clothes-peg on the nose, to train the nostrils to stay pinched in, like they use chin straps for children to make them sleep with their mouths shut.

There were some pegs on the line over the bath and I clipped one over my nose. But it hurt so much that my eyes started to water. I tried breathing in very deeply, to pull them into place by suction but that only made my eyes look wild, like an old racehorse on its last lap.

I examined the inside of my nose, to see if my polyps had shrunk a bit. They hadn't, and they were still purple.

He'd notice them if I were lying down, if we ever got that far and he'd be pretty disgusted. But at least the hairs weren't a problem. I could keep them trimmed, maybe I could even have the polyps removed, although that wouldn't stop the nostrils from flaring.

It was hopeless. I'd known that when I read the letter the first time. I couldn't spend the rest of my life breathing in deeply, even if it didn't make my eyes look wild.

There was nothing else for it. I tore the letter up and it was a great pity because he had sounded quite intelligent otherwise, and sensitive.

Too sensitive, maybe, letting noses worry him that much. Still, I consoled myself, if he was all that sensitive and even if my nose *were* perfect, there would probably be something else, something that he would get a thing about, sooner or later. One would have to be perfect all over to satisfy a man like that. Sooner or later something would revolt him, the way my breasts sagged, my flabby stomach, my appendix scar, my ears which stuck out a bit or my false teeth. I'd never know what was going to revolt him next.

And then I thought, maybe I should have put some of those defects in. Maybe it was misleading, just saying *Refined divorcée, age thirty-nine, teenage daughter, hazel eyes, brown hair, wishes to correspond with a view to, etc.* But if I had gone into details, about the flaring nostrils, prominent ears, flabby stomach and false teeth, who would reply?

Besides, I thought defensively, no one was perfect. *He* wouldn't be perfect, I was damn sure of that. And there would surely be other replies, more reasonable replies. They couldn't *all* be irregular. Not that I'd made up my mind about answering any of them. Or at least, I wasn't going to answer unless they were absolutely regular.

Girlie

I couldn't go to Dr Shaw but luckily before Mother and Gran could get really uptight about it the sickness stopped and Mother blamed it on the rum in Gran's tonic so Gran started watering her African violets with it because she said all the calcium and chicken scratchings in the eggshells were just like manure and Mother said no wonder I had been so sick and what was Gran trying to do, poison me?

They didn't talk to each other for a few hours after that and I knew they'd go on sitting in the lounge together so that each would know the other wasn't talking to her, and I was glad because at least it took their attention off me and I had the opportunity to read in the bedroom and find out what was happening without straining my eyes because the print of the book I'd got was terribly small, especially the footnotes, and the bathroom wasn't very well-lit.

I still had that picture in my mind of the awful pear that sounded like something from outer space, but it wasn't like that any more, I discovered. The limb buds had grown into arms, with hands and even tiny fingers.

I knew it wouldn't be those tiny fingers clawing at me inside. Those brand new little fingers would have been too weak yet to claw.

But the clawing was there all right, at the pit of my stomach, especially when I thought about Mother and Gran, about what they'd do if they really had something to worry about. That made the clawing a lot worse and I knew I had to stop thinking about Mother and Gran for the time being and just hope that Mother would keep her eyes on the lonely hearts column and Gran on the McKechnies and the cost of living for as long as possible, or until I could think of some way to make them see that having a baby if you're not even engaged isn't the end of the world which was going to be real hard because from time to time even I thought it was.

I could get over it by freeing my mind sometimes, repeating

a mantra until I was aching all over but I knew that withdrawal from the world of the senses was going to get pretty difficult when my stomach began to spill over into my lotus position.

Right thinking was the answer and in my situation I was beginning to learn that that meant not thinking at all until one absolutely had to. And then right thinking went with right living and we weren't living right, Mother and Gran and me, in that flat, not like Vern was, out in the open country which he said was always beautiful, even the dry areas with their acres and acres of aloes and prickly pears that flowered like the ringing of bells or the singing of a song.

Flowers sang, he said, with joy, like stars. He'd told me to read Blake and I tried but it didn't grab me much, except the songs like the one about the baby who was happy but had no name:

Sweet Joy I call thee, sweet joy befall thee ... I'd been able to remember that one because it rhymed, I think.

Vern could hear the flowers and the stars singing. If he'd been here I knew he would have said to me:

'Just keep still and listen to the baby growing.'

I did keep still but I couldn't hear anything. I didn't know how it would sound. Only Vern knew things like that.

5

Gran

Maybe Girlie *was* at an awkward age, but I had my problems too. There was Emily who came in every Friday morning to char, wash the kitchen and bathroom floors and clean the little bits of silver and brass that Iris had got as wedding presents. I felt all crowded out when she was there on a Friday, but getting down on my hands and knees to do floors was a bit beyond me at my age.

Lately, though, I could see there was something wrong with Emily. She was getting slower and slower. They always get slower and slower, of course, but she was getting slower than she should be getting and she moaned and groaned whenever she had to bend down and then she was off every end and side to the servant's lav right at the back of the block, so I had to ask: 'What's wrong with you, Emily?' and she said:

'It's my back, old Madam, that's sore and my perihod.'

'Well,' I said, 'it can't be the change of life, although it might be ...' because Emily is about forty and some women do start early.

'If it's the change of life,' I told her, 'there isn't anything you can do about it. We all have to go through that. Do you get hot flushes?'

She said: 'Old Madam?'

'Does it feel as if all your blood is rushing up to your head?' I asked her.

'No, old Madam,' she said. 'All my blood is rushing down to my legs.' And off she had to run to the lav again.

Well, it wasn't any good, she wasn't getting much done, so I asked the other women about it because Emily chars for three or four of us and they were all having the same trouble with her.

Mrs Goedhals thought she'd better go to the clinic, but I didn't know so much about that, about clinics.

'I'll give her something first and then we'll see,' I told them, because I know quite a bit about these things.

But when I came to think about it later I couldn't think of anything for bleeding except to put a cold key behind her neck, but that was for nosebleeds, or apply a tourniquet.

Then I thought, you can never go wrong with a tonic and luckily I still had some of that tonic that I'd made for Girlie that she wouldn't drink, so I gave it to Emily and told her to take three tablespoons a day, because it's a real strengthener, that tonic. I was sure it would strengthen the walls of her womb and help her over the change of life, if she was having the change of life, because people are more important than flowers and I could always get a bit of Fisons for the violets.

Mother

The business with Emily must have upset Gran. I could see she was in one of her moods as soon as we sat down to dinner.

'The water's flat,' she said, looking at me. When she isn't looking at me I can ignore her. It doesn't always pay in the long run though, so I said, to get it over with:

'What do you mean, the water's flat?'

'The water's flat is what I mean,' she said.

'What water?' In spite of myself I get a bit curious. Gran can be very irritating but the way her mind works never fails to amaze me.

'The water from the tap, of course,' she said. 'Really Iris!'

'Oh,' I said. 'How peculiar. I've heard of beer going flat, but I've never heard …'

'There's a lot you haven't heard,' Gran said. 'Doesn't mean it isn't so just because you've never heard it.'

'Well, how do you know?' I asked her.

'Because it's got a flat taste, of course,' she said. 'They've put too much chlorine in it again.'

'You mean fluoridation?' I asked, not knowing what I meant myself, exactly.

'If I'd meant that,' Gran said, 'I would have said so, wouldn't I?'

'They only put chlorine in swimming pools as far as I know,' I said.

'Well, that's as far as you know, I'm glad you have the grace to admit it.'

'Oh, really, Gran,' I said.

'Yes, really,' she said. 'But that doesn't make the water more …'

'Efferescent?' I suggested.

'Now don't you go getting on your high horse,' she said. 'All I meant was that the water tastes like food that's got no salt in it. No need to make a thing of it.'

'I wasn't,' I said. 'But water's got no taste.'

'Course it's got a taste,' she said. 'Put a blindfold on and you'd know the difference between water and ginger beer or tomato soup. And I say this water's flat because it tastes like flat water.'

'Oh well,' I said, and I began to gather up the plates. 'It'll do for washing the dishes I suppose.'

Washing dishes always makes me morbid, and I thought, that's it, the story of my life. Long pointless conversations about things like flat water. Would *Mister X* take that, I wondered, or *Viking*, and still have a sense of humour?

And the trouble was, at thirty-nine it's just about irrevocable. Maybe twelve is irrevocable too, and thirteen; but thirty-nine is a watershed, from there you can only slide down, sagging all over.

I must have sighed heavily because Gran heard me right in the lounge and came to ask what I thought I had to sigh about. I couldn't go into all that so I said nothing, and then she said:

'Esmé McKechnie was talking about your letter the other

day.'

I swung around so fast that I splashed soapy water all over the lino. 'My what?' I asked.

'She was just chatting,' Gran said. 'There was a parcel for Mrs Retief from Stutterheim as well, she said, and I said the post isn't what it used to be, like the buses "Well, at least Iris got something," she said, and she looked at me. She's just like a little black crow, you know. If I didn't happen to like Esmé McKechnie I really wouldn't have anything to do with her. But I didn't let on, I just said it was a pen pal.'

'And that shut her up?' I asked.

'Oh, Esmé's sharp,' Gran said. 'No flies on her. "Pen pals are a good thing," she says. "You can learn all sorts of things from all over the world." Once she was corresponding with someone in Rome, she said but *your* letter had got a Port Elizabeth postmark on it, and "what's the good of a pen pal in the same place?" she said. "Nothing you can learn from it." That gave me quite a turn because I know you don't want everybody to know about it, so to cover up I asked her if she's heard about this flat neurosis thing that's going round.'

I gritted my teeth. 'There's nothing to cover up,' I said, but Gran just went on:

' "Everything's so crowded today," I told Esmé, to put her in her place. "No room to swing a dead cat in without hitting last year's Christmas cake." Then she started insinuating that your late father didn't love me because he didn't sing me romantic songs when he was full of pots like old Mac did, and I told her your late father didn't get full of pots, all he ever took was a drop of cooking sherry, but she was really only fed up because I wouldn't tell her anything about your letter, you know, about whether it was bad news or good news or who it was from. She thought I was trying to hide something.'

I jerked the plug out of the basin so hard it nearly broke the chain. 'Well, you certainly did your best to give her that impression,' I said. 'And you want to know what I've got to sigh about?'

'Count your blessings,' Gran said, and then mercifully it was time for her radio quiz.

Girlie was in our room so I went to the bathroom to sit down and have a cigarette in private. If I had the money I'd buy Gran a bedside radio so I could sit in the lounge for a change without having to listen to a quiz or to what Esmé McKechnie said, which would be a whole lot more elegant than having to sit on a lav all the time, and I sighed again but Gran didn't hear me because the door was closed and she'd got the radio on so loud it was making the crockery in the kitchen rattle.

Girlie

Once I'd stopped throwing up I felt fine, except that it worried me, what Mother and Gran were going to say when they knew and I wondered, how am I ever going to tell them?

I tried to imagine it. Gran would be listening to her quiz like now and I'd come in and say: 'By the way, Gran, I'm going to have a baby,' and she'd glare at me and say 'Shhhhh! Ah, now I'll never know! He's just said *exactly* how many decorated pieces of bamboo and ivory were formerly used in mah-jong! Now, what were you saying?'

Or Gran wouldn't be listening to her quiz, she'd be leaning over to pat my hand and she'd say: 'Come, have a little word with your Gran now, my gel, tell your Gran all the little things you've been doing.' And I'd never be able to tell her the little things I'd been doing, not when she put it like that, and certainly not the consequences of it. It would give her a stroke.

Or Mother coming home from work saying: 'Your tan's lasting well. I wish I'd been able to have a little fun on the beach.' How would I be able to tell her then? They'd both have strokes.

They'd never understand that it wasn't like they'd think it

was and I wouldn't ever be able to explain it to them, and even if I tried it would have to come in Vern's words and I'd never get them right, they'd all be jumbled, like if I tried to explain about fate or the Moirae and having to let things be, the way Vern did that day when the sea was getting choppy and grey and the beach tide-marked with brown scum and seaweed and the tufts of yellow grass on the dunes were doubled over in the wind and I knew there wasn't much time left although I couldn't believe he was really going to go, just like Gran and Mother won't believe things they don't want to believe.

I remember Vern talking about Lachesis who assigned the term of one's life, about Clotho who weaves the pattern of one's destiny and someone else, I couldn't remember, who cut the threads or rather the thread, he said, because there was only one continuous thread of life called advaita, and we were all part of it.

Everything in the universe, he said, at any given moment, participates with everything else that shares that same unit of time, and he said Jung had also said that and it was true, only now that truth was being buried under concrete and tarmac and reinforced steel, clouded over and choked with smog and drowned out by the groaning and grinding of machines.

He said a lot of other things too, about how karma, which was duty or desire, had to be right, in obedience to dharma, the nature of things. But if I tried to tell all that to Mother she'd get impatient and say, get to the point, and the *point* was the thing that was going to give her a stroke if she knew.

Vern wasn't there to help me, so I got the sheet of Tagore's poetry he'd given me, but the one I happened to read first, *Do not go, my love* brought back all the pain because the last lines: *Could I but entangle your feet with my heart and hold them fast to my breast* made me see him again, walking down that long road away from me.

Gran

After the quiz I caught Iris helping herself to another gin and that always gets on my nerves.

'You'll want to watch your liver,' I told her, so of course she ups and rolls her eyes and sighs.

'What are you sighing yourself silly for all the time?' I asked her. 'What have you got to sigh about? Just be thankful that you're not the butcher's wife. *She's* got something to sigh about if anyone has.'

'And what has she got to sigh about?' Iris asks. She can never take my word for anything.

'Well, that poor woman,' I told her, 'I don't know how she puts up with it, I asked her and she said it goes back a long time, to when they were in school together and he had scurvy heels.'

The way Iris has taken to looking at me lately I'll swear she's trying to find signs that I'm going senile, but she's got a hope, because my mind is as sharp as a razor blade, always has been.

'Well,' she says, 'has he still got scurvy heels, or what?'

'I don't know,' I told her. 'She wasn't complaining about his heels, she was just mentioning it, like a person mentions things when you let the conversation run naturally; and I've never seen his heels. He always wears shoes in the shop. Maybe he doesn't at home, I don't know.'

'If all she's got to worry about,' Iris says, 'is his scurvy heels, then ...'

'It's not that,' I told her. 'It's his sleeping.'

'Oh for God's sake, Gran,' she says, blaspheming again. Iris is always getting impatient these days. She can't let the conversation run naturally, taking its own course, like Esmé McKechnie. And there's another one who has had real troubles in her time, that Iris ought to be thinking about and count herself lucky.

'What I'm saying is that he sleeps all the time,' I told her, 'except when he's in the shop. At least I've never seen him sleep in the shop and I go in every day. But she says he gets home and says, "Wake me for supper," and then he sleeps in the chair until she wakes him and after supper he says he's tired and goes straight to bed. Now how would you like that? And *she's* gone and bought herself a wig.'

'A *wig*?' Iris asks, like she's never heard of such a thing.

'Yes,' I said. 'She's married to a man who sleeps all the time and she still cares enough to go and buy herself a wig. Now there's courage for you.'

'So what do you want *me* to do?' Iris asks. 'Go and buy myself a wig?'

Iris is always missing the point these days. On purpose too, I'm beginning to think. 'I'm saying *she's* got something to *worry* about,' I said. 'And she still buys herself a *wig*.'

'Well, *she's* got a husband, even if he does sleep all the time,' Iris says. '*And* a wig. What have *I* got?'

I got annoyed at that, because some people are never satisfied. Some people don't *want* to know how lucky they are.

'Well, wigs are easy,' I said. 'You can always buy yourself a *wig* if you want one.'

'You think I should buy myself a wig?' Iris asks. 'Is that what you're saying?'

'No!' I said, and I honestly don't know where I was getting the patience from. 'What do *you* want a wig for? You've got a perfectly good head of hair, like me. You take after me there, and you should be grateful for it.'

'Well, what are you going on about wigs for then?' she asks. Iris is my own daughter but sometimes I can't get through to her at all. 'I'm only *saying*,' I said, 'that it's a sign of courage.'

'All right!' she says. 'So wigs are a sign of courage. So maybe if I had some courage I'd buy myself a wig, but I don't *need* a wig because I've got a good head of hair. So where does that get me?'

I gave up then and went to bed, because some people just won't learn to count their blessings and I have to say it, even if she is my own daughter.

6

Mother

I saw the letter as soon as I came in, propped up against the china Pekinese on the telephone table. Gran didn't say anything, not even hello, she just sat on the settee with her knee-blanket around her because of the cold.

'Where's Girlie?' I asked and she grumped and looked away.

Good, I thought, if Girlie hadn't come in yet I wouldn't have to read my correspondence in the lav which wasn't elegant whichever way you looked at it. I took it very calmly, even to the extent of searching all over for the letter-opener I knew I had somewhere but when I couldn't find it and couldn't contain my curiosity any longer I had to tear it open which wasn't all that elegant either.

There was a preamble about how nice I sounded and how much he wanted to correspond with a view to, etc., and then he asked point-blank:

Why did you get divorced? He had to know, he said, if I was the innocent party because he had been; his ex-wife had been the guilty party on account of her drinking:

... and I mean a real drinker, alcoholic, if you want to call it that. Brandy on the pantry shelf behind the bottles of canned beans and carrots. Oh, she was a great canner, my wife, give the devil his due, always canning things, only she was always getting canned herself. Ha! Ha! (get it?). It was for cooking, she said, I mean the brandy, for stews and things, only she was always getting stewed herself (Ha! Ha!). After that she hid it in the garage. It took me all my time trying to find where she was hiding it. The only trouble was the place is full of hiding places, I couldn't follow her all the time to find out where she was hiding it so I had to give up. I hope

*you don't drink. I've been put right off myself, so if you do, don't
bother to answer because I just can't stand the smell of the stuff
any more.*

Well, I thought, he had a sense of humour all right, only I
didn't feel like laughing, because just then, at that precise
moment, I needed a drink badly. Association of ideas, or
something. Auto-suggestion. I was pretty strung up but I
forced myself to consider the matter calmly, and I thought no,
I'm not a *real* drinker. I only need it sometimes because of Gran
and Girlie and feeling lonely and feeling my life isn't leading
anywhere and wondering what I'm going to do with myself
when Gran is gone and Girlie is married because I wouldn't
live with Girlie, I swore, bringing my pots and pans and sheets
and cutlery in exchange for company, and yet, I suppose, if
the worst came to the worst, I'd leave it to Girlie and not quite
leave it to Girlie, like Gran had left it to me, while not quite
leaving it to me, because when a girl is happy, in love, getting
married, she tends to be generous, she wants everyone else to
be happy too, especially her own mother …

I stopped myself in mid-sigh in case Gran heard me, and
I thought, it's mostly because of her, when she starts arching
her eyebrow at me I generally begin to need a drink. And I
know from experience that if I can't have it, I begin to need
it badly. Especially if I'm being followed and sniffed at all the
time … like he would probably do, even worse than Gran.

Better forget it, I told myself. Besides, his wife must have
had a good reason for drinking; he probably wasn't as innocent
as he liked to think. That made me feel a bit better, or at least
less of how bad I was feeling, and I decided to write another
advert, but this time after *enjoys outings, cinema and dancing* I
would add, frankly, *and an occasional drink.* That should sort
that one out, I hoped, and I went through to the lounge.

'Girlie not back yet?' I asked. 'Well, I think I'll have a little
drink then.'

'In *this* weather?' Gran said.

41

'What's the weather got to do with it?' I asked. 'It's nearly six o'clock.'

'Time's no excuse,' Gran said.

'Well, she always gets back before ...'

'For *drinking!*' Gran snapped.

'Drinking?' At that the disappointment of the letter bore down on me again, but gin does that too, gives you a lift and then dumps you. I got all bitter and turned on Gran:

'Don't you start in on me now,' I told her. 'It's one thing to *drink* and quite another to have a little drink when you need it. And I do, doing a man's job and being nattered and nagged at all the time. Nobody's *perfect!* What the hell do you expect?'

Gran nodded, her eyes all sharp like when she knows she's on to something. 'So that's how it is,' she said. 'But then I warned you didn't I? The sort of men who have to advertise themselves ...'

'All right!' I cried. 'So you've said. They're irregular. But what's wrong with having an occasional drink I'd like to know?'

'*Socially,*' Gran said. 'Socially it's all right. But when you start in on your own ...'

'I'm not on my own,' I said. 'I'm with you.' And I nearly said, worse luck!

'A social *occasion,*' Gran said.

At that I sat down and closed my eyes. 'What social occasion do I ever have?' I asked her.

'Iris, you're not too old,' Gran said, starting in on one of her 'talking- to's', 'to take a bit of advice from your mother. Seek ye first the Kingdom of Heaven, because as long as you go on hankering after ...'

I couldn't help it. I just started weeping quietly, my tears splashing into my glass.

'What's all *this* now?' Gran asked, and just then Girlie came in.

'Where the hell have *you* been?' I sobbed.

Girlie stood staring at me.

'Just because I have a little drink,' I moaned.

'She's tired,' Gran said, heaving herself up. 'Your mother's tired. It's the weather. Make her a nice cup of tea, there's a good gel. Come on now, Iris,' she said to me. 'Pull yourself together. If you keep a hold of yourself you'll find you won't go all to pieces like this.' She took the glass out of my hand and I let her lead me to the bedroom like a child.

'Just you lie down now,' she said. 'And forget all about it. Stop hankering, and remember you've got Girlie and me to care about you.'

Maybe she thought that would make me feel better and maybe it should have, but somehow it didn't, not even when Girlie brought the tea in, all weak and slopped in the saucer, and said with real concern:

'Don't let it bug you, Mother, whatever it is.'

I said: 'No.' And I thought, I must put more orange juice with it. Nearly neat gin's a real drag.

Gran

I made salmon rissoles for dinner, but with pilchards because of the cost of living, mashing them up with potatoes, a pinch of mixed herbs, to just one egg and a little flour for binding, measuring it all out into pats to make three each and four left over for lunch when Girlie came in from her lectures. I like us to have a proper dinner, sitting down. None of this eating sandwiches off the kitchen unit business, and I always say grace because I believe it binds us together, just like egg binds the flour and fish, although I must say they were very absent-minded about it, especially Girlie. More often than not these days I had to remind her to close her eyes and lately I've even had to remind her to open them again. If she weren't so young I'd swear she had something on her mind.

It's a terrible shame, and not from any want of example

and instruction on my part either. Iris has had every advantage given her but you'd never have thought it, the way she was off every end and side writing to bleeding hearts men. What she needs, I thought, is to take a good long look at herself and face facts, like that she's nearly forty with a daughter nearly grown, a figure that's not what it was and mouse-brown eyes for all that she likes to call them hazel; she should realise that there's not much left for her but religion and act accordingly.

But I've done my best, she's long over twenty-one and I can't go on being responsible for her soul. I've got my own to worry about, especially now, at my time of life. Not that you have to be a fanatic about it. Keep it to yourself, I always say, but a little bit of religion never did anyone any harm.

I sometimes think if it wasn't for me Girlie wouldn't have had any instruction or example at all. I've never heard Iris and Frank setting her on the right path, and that's another thing about the Catholics, they do drum that catechism into their children until they don't know whether they're coming or going and if *they* lapse they know they'll be sent straight to hell, no nonsense about it, or that other place they've got in between.

So it was up to me as usual, but I've often wondered what was the use of all the instruction I've tried to give that gel, the way she was sitting mooning around under those heathen pictures with her lips moving, not that she was praying either. You can't pray to God sitting flat on your bottom like that. It isn't respectful. Even Girlie knows that. I sometimes think she's deaf and we don't know it, but when I say 'Girlie!' she says 'Yes Gran', as meek as a lamb, so I can see she just wasn't listening.

She used to go to Sunday School when she was small, in her little frock and little hat, like Little Bo-Peep, but they don't even wear hats any more, except the older people who've still got some respect.

It really is getting to be a godless world, just like Esmé McKechnie says, but she's all right, she's a Catholic and they're stricter about these things than our lot, or they know they can forget about heaven and maybe the middle place too, it all depends on the size of the sin.

I don't believe in praying to Mary and all those saints but when you start giving in on little sins the big ones start slipping past you too. Some of these young ministers are even wondering if there's a hell these days, but if you start wondering about hell you go on to wondering about heaven and then there's no point left in anything before you know where you are.

The Catholics are sensible enough not to start wondering about anything. They're told exactly where they stand so no one's going to pull the rug out from under *their* feet, although Esmé says that last Pope of theirs was a bit of a rug-puller.

The rissoles were nearly done when Iris came in with another parcel. I knew what it was even before she opened it up and I thought yes, here I am trying to make ends meet, making salmon rissoles with pilchards and she's out buying more threads to hang on her back.

'It's a nasty colour Iris,' I said when she showed it to me.

'It's not so bad,' she says. 'It was on a sale. I got it cheap.'

'Well, it looks it,' I said, and she gets all snappy:

'It's my money,' she says.

I could see we were in for a bit of a tiff, and sometimes it's a good thing, it clears the air. Iris has been a bit strung up lately, she needed to blow off a bit of steam, and my own feelings were a bit pent up too, what with Emily and one thing and another, so I reminded her:

'Not all of it. What about my pension?'

'Your pension!' she sneers, and I could see that she really was in a nasty mood, which must have been why she bought that horrible dress which she must be regretting now.

'Your pension is hardly enough for your snuff,' she says. I thought that was going too far, but then she went even further: 'And while we're on snuff,' she says, 'when you go poking through my drawers try not to sneeze on the wall. There are

45

brown spots like fly dirt all over the wall.'

'Oh,' I said, 'are there? Well, that's exactly what they are. They *are* fly dirt. I told you Emily can't get around the walls these days. And anyway I still say it's a horrible colour. Makes you look like you've got TB.'

I was really upset. It didn't clear the air at all. I've spoilt her, I thought, made a rod for my own back. I didn't even feel like giving them the rissoles then and I would have thrown them in the bin if it wasn't such a sin to waste food.

Girlie

I really expected desire to go when you're pregnant, but it doesn't and sometimes I nearly freaked out, just remembering how it was, like when Vern was teasing me, or maybe he just wanted to be sure that I really wanted him because Vern was like that. He'd laugh and say: 'You're pinching me, I'm going to end up with a blue backside like an ancient Briton ...'

It was no good feeling like that now so I tried to think of the 'product of conception' as the book called it, reminding me of a production line consumer thing, and I didn't know how they could be so insensitive, the people who wrote those books.

He would have developed palmprints by now, faint fine delicate lines like Vern's, perhaps. He'd have eyelids too, and I saw them half closed in that sleepy, peaceful look of Vern's that saw all the beauty in every little thing, how the earth expanded with joy as the sun warmed it, or how a little breeze rustling up off the veld would animate the moon's cartoons of trees, and shrubs against the skyline.

Remembering the way he told it I really could feel a part of all that without the help of any images or mantras. But perhaps that didn't count, skipping a step like that, and not losing desire first.

In any case it was gone, that feeling of peace, a minute

later when I read: *Generally considered the best time for abortions.*
I went rigid, seeing those tiny fine palmprints again, and some
of the other things that Vern had told me about, that weren't
beautiful at all, like the little creatures steamrollered flat on the
road in the early morning light, little rock rabbits, meerkats
and tortoises, plastered down in their own blood.

Mother

I should have been able to laugh, but I couldn't because all I
could think was that something was wrong, but I didn't know
what.

My advert had been perfectly normal and ordinary. I
hadn't even stipulated a car like some of the others did, or
warned off chancers and miniskirt and fortune hunters. But
I was attracting all the kooks and cranks in creation. Or were
they just testing my sense of humour?

I reread the letter:

*It was after she got the pictures that the trouble started, you know,
those pin-ups from the 30s that you used to buy at the OK, tall
thin women with frizzy blonde hair and skin like paper and those
long dresses that cling right down to the knees and then flare out,
with their thin red lips and baby-blue eyes, and she, my ex-wife,
was fat with missing teeth and straight hair and a yellow skin. I
was used to that, you understand, and I didn't mind, but she went
on diet and permed her hair to a frizz and bleached it so that it
looked like coir and then she got a plate with four front teeth in it.
As you can imagine all this cost a lot of money and I said to her,
why get four front teeth? Because the rest of them were bound to
go some day and then she'd want a full set, so why pay for four
teeth now and a full set again later, why not wait until they all
go rotten and then get a full set, but no, she had to have the four
front teeth, and we haven't got money to waste so we broke up over*

47

those four teeth. I know it sounds like a small thing but you've heard about the last straw, so I hope you're not extravagant in a likewise manner because I swore on the day of the divorce that I'll never buy another tooth as long as I live, so if you haven't got a good set of teeth, strong and healthy that's likely to last, or your own set of false teeth, paid for and all, there will be no point in us corresponding with a view to anything, because when I swear something I always stick to it.

No, I thought, he means it all right. There's one man the dentists are not going to make a fortune out of. And that left me exactly nowhere. I wondered whether I should draft another advert and cancel the old one. But if I said something like *people who are obsessed with noses, drinking and teeth need not reply* – *I'd* sound like a kook.

So I decided to leave my advert as it was, and one day, surely, one of those sincere, honest, tall gentlemen in an executive position, with house, car and welcomes encumbrances would reply and ask me to a club dance. One had to believe that.

In the meantime I knew I had to tear the letter up, because even though I did happen to have my own set of false teeth, paid for and all, I might need something else one day, a wooden leg or a glass eye or something, you never know, and where would that get me? Another divorce.

7

Gran

Emily wasn't getting around the floors at all any more, let alone the walls, so I told her to take four tablespoons of the tonic and have faith, but when she brought the empty consol jar back and said she still wasn't feeling any better and she was getting thin too, which was funny because we all made a good thick stew or a curry on the days she came to us, I spoke to Esmé McKechnie and Mrs Goedhals and we decided that she'd better go to the clinic, but then we had a good deal of trouble deciding which day.

'Friday is always a bad day at the clinic,' I told them when they said she'd better go at the end of the week. 'Because it's the end of the week they have to queue up for hours.'

Mrs Goedhals said Wednesday was a bad day too and Esmé said Thursday was even worse because most of them get their time off on a Thursday and then those who didn't go to the church meetings had nowhere to go but the clinic, so we finally decided on a Tuesday and Mrs Goedhals said she would tell Mrs Merriman that Emily was going on her day because Tuesday was the best day but the rest of us would share a bit of time with her if she wanted anything done.

I told Emily she'd got to go to the clinic and stop playing around with her health because one never knew, it could be cancer and she said yes, it felt like cancer because her legs were like lead and her back weighted down with bricks and the headaches and the sweating.

Of course, that was why she didn't have the strength to get around the floors, she was sweating all her strength out, and I thought it was just as well that we made her go to the clinic, but, would you believe it, instead of going to the clinic she went to some Indian down in South End who called himself a doctor and he gave her an injection and a bottle of green muti that looked as if it had been scooped off the top of a slimy pond.

I was good and annoyed at her for wasting Mrs Merriman's time and money like that, but Emily just stood there grinning at me as if her backache had finally turned her mind.

'Well, what did he say? Did he examine you down there?' I couldn't help being suspicious about the whole thing because of the way she was grinning at me.

Oh yes, she says, he examined her all over. He always did, she said, 'just to be sure, even when your foot is sore or your eye.'

'Well then, what did he say?' I asked because I couldn't for the life of me see what there was to be so cheerful about. And then she told me she was going to have a baby. Grinning like all get-out. Her time was not past, she said, and now, when he saw the baby, her boyfriend would marry her at last.

'Oh,' I said, and I didn't really believe it, not at her age, but still, one never knew. Emily had been praying about it for years. She'd even asked me to pray about it but I told her to get married first otherwise it would be a terrible sin for me even to pray about it. But of course they've got different ideas, and maybe God takes all that into account.

'I can't congratulate you on the baby until you're married,' I told her. 'It wouldn't be right for me to do it because I'm supposed to know better. Now, what about your job?'

She would carry on working for a while, she said, because she needed the money now that she was getting married and having a baby. Well, that was all right, I told her, because it would give us a little while to look out for someone else, but I advised her to get married as soon as possible because now she'd been told it wasn't right, she also knew better and she wouldn't have any excuse any more.

Mother

'I don't much like the look of Girlie,' Gran said to me, pinching her lips in like she always does when there's something she doesn't like.

'But you've always said she was the spitting image of you,' I reminded her. 'It's a bit late now to ...'

'You know what I mean,' Gran said. 'The way she's mooning around these days with that fishy look in her eyes.'

'Fishy look?'

'Like they're under water.'

I knew exactly what she meant. Girlie did look as if she was living in a different element from us and it was beginning to get on my nerves.

'Do you think she's sickening for something?' I asked, because Gran sees more of Girlie than I do and she'd notice the slightest signs of illness, start ferreting out the symptoms and doctoring away.

'I *thought* she was,' Gran said, very slowly, 'that time she had the upset tummy, when I made that tonic up for her.'

'But she didn't take it,' I said. I have to be very careful with Gran. She tends to go at it like a witchdoctor and I never know what she's going to decide to 'make up' next. 'You haven't been giving her anything else, have you?'

'No,' Gran said, still very slowly and unlike her. 'But she's acting very strange these days. Tells me about how everything is an illusion, a *maya* or something like that. She said even the tonic was *maya* although it tasted like rotten eggs. It's making me wonder if what's ailing her is, well, normal. I'm wondering ... you know I never thought Frank was altogether ... and these things can be inherited. After all, how can a tonic be *maya*? A tonic is a tonic.'

'Oh *that*,' I said. 'That's just one of these fads. She's supposed to be meditating and all that. They're all doing it these days. Next year it will be something else.'

'Well, if that's what's making her look so fishy,' Gran said, 'you'd be better putting your foot down. It smacks altogether too much of false gods to me and it's affecting her. It's your duty, Iris, before she lands up in the outer darkness.'

'If I stop her she'll think it's more important than it is,' I said. 'And it's not. Frankly, I think it's that boyfriend of hers. He started her on all this. She probably thinks she's in love with him.'

'In love with who?' Gran almost shouted. 'A child like Girlie? In love?'

'For heaven's sake Gran, it's not serious,' I told her. 'It's probably just a crush. Everyone goes through it. I'm just thinking aloud, anyway. She did change a bit after she met that boy.'

'What boy?' Gran asked. It began to annoy me, the way she was making such a thing of it, acting as if Girlie had been ravaged or something. 'Oh, you know,' I said. 'That peculiar, quiet, long-haired boy, what was his name? She only brought him in once or twice. I can't say he made much of an impression on me, I never even caught his name. They met on the beach, sometimes, at the weekends, don't you remember?'

'*That* boy!' Gran yelled. 'I'll say I remember. They were going to the cinema and she went in jeans! She doesn't dress like a little lady, Iris, and I'm warning you. Now I come to think of it, he didn't look much of a little gentleman to me either. I remember warning you at the time. He doesn't look much of a little gentleman to me, I remember saying to you at the time.'

'All right!' I said. 'He wouldn't look like the sort of little gentleman you would remember from God knows when, Gran. Times change.'

'The more's the pity then,' Gran said. 'Change isn't always a good thing, Iris. You'll come to realise the truth of that when you're older.'

'All right,' I said.

'And now you've got Girlie sitting around in that abject, unnatural sort of way, what I want to know is, what are you going to do about it?'

'All right!' I said. 'I'm going to talk to her. She hasn't been out since last summer, now I come to think of it. They must have had a tiff, broken up or something, and she's upset, naturally. Just don't make a thing of it and she'll realise it's nothing. She's young. At her age there are plenty more fish in the sea.'

'At her age she shouldn't even be thinking about fish,' Gran said.

'Just leave it to me,' I told her. 'I'll sort it all out.'

So while we were busy getting the supper, I said to Girlie, very casually:

'Whatever happened to that … what was his name, that friend of yours, the one who looked sleepy, that you met on the beach?'

Girlie hesitated. 'Who?' she asked.

'You know,' I said. 'I think he was a life-saver. He was rather a quiet boy.'

'I don't know,' she said. 'And he wasn't exactly a *boy*, Mother.'

'Oh,' I said. And then Gran chipped in, after I'd told her to leave it to me:

'And how would you be knowing? Not that it's important, because there's plenty of time yet for *that* sort of thing, my gel, as I've told you before and one day you'll be thanking me for it when a nice, neat, clean, young gentle …'

Girlie dropped the cheese she was grating and walked out of the kitchen.

'I *told* you to leave it to me,' I said to Gran. 'Maybe she's more upset about him than we thought. She's a sensitive girl and she's at an awkward age.'

'Upset about *him*?' Gran said. '*I* remember him, he'd got his hair down about his ears like a spaniel. He'd got a bell around his neck like a cow and old tyres on his feet! It's all coming back to me.'

'They weren't just old tyres,' I said. 'They were sandals made from old tyres. It's just the fashion. Next year it will be something else, maybe even dark suits again, and socks and polished shoes. You can't judge a person by what he's got on his feet.'

'Oh yes you can,' Gran said. 'When they're old tyres you can ...'

I left it at that. My heart just wasn't in it. I couldn't help preferring polished shoes to old tyres myself. Even if they were supposed to be sandals. And the bell around his neck didn't help much either. It didn't make him look very dependable. It'd never get him a good, steady, executive job, with a house and a car. And I began to wonder whether Girlie was going to have the same sort of luck that I had, attracting all the kooks and cranks in creation.

Girlie

I didn't let it bug me. I just preferred not to talk about Vern to them, because all they would ever notice about him would be his sandals and his long hair. A lot of it was too private to explain anyway. It belonged to us, and how we'd felt, like floating, wrapped around with, cotton wool clouds, all the hard hang-ups forgotten. How could I explain it to them?

I couldn't explain the things Vern used to talk about either, because I didn't understand a lot of it myself, although I tried to listen carefully. Some of it must have sunk in like hypnotism or learning from records during sleep, because I remembered odd, unrelated parts, about McLuhan who said mysticism is tomorrow's science dreamed today, about the Piscean Age of Tears and the murder of Christ and the new Age of Aquarius, the end of disillusionment and the reawakening of faith.

And all those philosophers who Vern said had tripped over Hegel's line of despair, admitting their limitations now, rubbing out their fuzzy patterns and throwing away the old templates because they wouldn't ever fit, they'd ignored too much of the truth, or tried to ignore that part that couldn't be intellectualised, or systematised or even expressed in words.

You couldn't ever make the right pattern until you know all the parts, Vern said, and no one knows all the parts because we're dimensional, and truth isn't.

Vern might have been able to explain all that to them, and they would've seen there was a whole lot more to him than sandals and long hair. But I doubted it. Mother would have got bored and Gran would have started to argue as she always did when there was something she didn't understand.

Then I remembered how Vern had explained about us being dimensional and I thought, that made it easier, maybe they'd understand that, as a starting point, so I went back to the kitchen where Gran was still grumbling about how young I was and I said:

'To get down to basics, imagine a worm confined between two panes of glass, living its whole life without any conception that there is a third dimension, so although it doesn't know, that doesn't stop the third from existing, does it? So the worm has to take it on faith.'

Mother smiled vaguely at me, and said: 'Is this for Biology?'

Gran wouldn't even look at me. 'Worms can't have faith because they haven't got souls,' she said.

And I thought, well, having faith isn't an easy thing, it's about as difficult as meditating and maybe it's all a hangover still, from the line of despair, and the Age of Tears.

8

Mother

Gran glared sideways at me and sucked her lips in. 'There's another letter come,' she said.

It wasn't next to the Pekinese. 'Where have you hidden it this time?' I asked her, and I went to the kitchen, to check on the marmalade. 'Gran!' I called. 'I'm not in the mood for this sort of ...'

She came to stand at the door.

'You know, Iris,' she said, 'I'm beginning to think you *have* got it.'

'How can *I* have it?' I cried. 'I wasn't here when it came!'

'No,' she said. 'I mean this flat thing. This flat business. This neurosis. You *are* getting irritable all the time. And these fits of temper about nothing. How have you been sleeping lately?'

I could have screamed. 'What does it matter how I've been sleeping? All I want is my letter!'

'Well, there's no need to shout at *me* about it,' Gran said. 'Or about any of the others. *I* didn't write them and if they don't come up to scratch remember I warned you ...'

'All right,' I said. 'All right! I'll find it myself.' I flung through to the bedroom to put my bag down and there it was, propped against the ashtray next to my bed.

'For God's sake!' I said. Girlie was mumbling something that sounded like *bootsoo*, sitting on her bed with her knees stuck out like a crippled grasshopper's.

'Go on and help Gran with the supper or something,' I told her. 'Get some exercise, for God's sake!'

I waited for her to uncoil herself and shuffle out before I opened the letter.

A small photograph fell out – *recent snap will be appreciated* I'd said – showing him sitting behind a huge desk, two telephones at his elbow and wearing horn-rimmed spectacles which were just right for his heavy square face. He was looking directly at the camera, sincerely and honestly, and obviously from a good executive position. I couldn't see anything irregular about him. In fact, he looked so marvellously regular that I nearly tore the letter trying to open it.

He was a widower, in his late forties, I read, in a managerial position, fond of films, dancing, outings of all kinds and good books. He lived in a big flat on the beachfront, and he was very lonely, having been plagued in the past and taken for numerous rides by various fortune hunters.

I felt so weak I had to sit down. That's all right, I told myself, that's quite all right. Because I wasn't a fortune hunter. All I wanted was sincere, honest companionship, to go to the films, dancing and all those other outings. I'd even offer to go on working to prove it.

Best of all, he was not interested in beauty, as such. *A loving personality, a sense of humour and an even temper* were all that mattered to him, because, he wrote:

> *My late wife had an erratic, ungovernable temper, she was subject to fleeting changes of mood that had nothing to do with what I said or did or had omitted to say or do. I was almost grateful the day I buried her, I'm ashamed to admit, but you will understand why I am looking, above all, for someone with an even temper.*

That was all right, it was fine, I told myself. I had a very even temper, basically. And if I had any changes of mood they had very definitely to do with what someone said or did, like Girlie's rambling about boots and worms, or Gran hiding my letters. My moods weren't really erratic at all. I was always being sorely provoked.

But I decided to be very careful. I'd have a drink and think very carefully about how best, how most subtly, to convey my loving personality, my sense of humour, my even temper and the fact that I was anything but a fortune hunter. I wouldn't even mention his managerial position. I'd ignore that as though I hadn't even noticed it and he could be a street-sweeper for all I cared. I wasn't sure how best to convey an even temper in a letter, though, so I decided to cross that bridge later.

In the meantime I'd be light and humorous: *I'm anything but beautiful!* No, that was putting it too strongly. *You know what they say: beauty is in the eye of the beholder!* Something like that. And I'd have to be especially subtle and humorous about Gran and Girlie: *There's my mother, just passing her threescore years and ten!* Would that sound callous? He had been pretty forthright himself about burying his wife. But no, of course I didn't want to bury Gran, I'd rather she went into a Home, or anywhere, as long as she didn't spoil everything by forcing tonics on him, or burning eau de cologne next to his head, like she did with Frank.

And Girlie: *There's my daughter, very mature at eighteen* (she was quiet, anyway) *who has had a special boyfriend for some little while now ...* But of course, she didn't have him any more, which was just as well, now I came to think of it, because I couldn't see that bell and those dirty toenails going down very well with the sort of executive who wore horn-rims and had two telephones.

Maybe it would be better to wait a few days. Collect my thoughts. It wouldn't do to reply right away in any case, and appear too eager. I'd keep busy for a few days, be calm, even-tempered, develop my loving personality and sense of humour as far as possible with Gran around and try to see the light, bright, funny side of Girlie's peculiarities too. It shouldn't be too impossible, at least not now that I had the letter and the chance, perhaps, of making a new life, one never knew ...

Calm and even-tempered, I lit a cigarette and went to Gran in the lounge. I didn't want to say anything too soon, for fear of tempting fate, but it just came out:

'By the way Gran, I was reading about a charity group that goes around to all the Old Folks Homes, giving them hairdos and manicures, massages and facials ...'

Gran just looked at me so I raised my voice a bit because she could sometimes make me feel guilty just by looking at me: 'Apparently they have a gay old time of it, quite a social gathering while they're waiting their turn, and they're all the same age and have a lot in common.'

'Ah well,' Gran said. 'I've always been lucky that way, having a good head of hair. All I've ever needed is a hairnet.'

I hung on to my even temper. 'The hair-do's and facials make the old ladies feel young again,' I said. 'One said it took years off her.'

'Take more than a facial to take years off me,' Gran said. 'Never had much time for creams and pomades and things. There's nothing like soap and water, as I keep having to tell Girlie. Catch me sitting there like a poodle, waiting to be trimmed and trotted out!'

The trouble was that Gran knew I wasn't really serious about it. I just couldn't see her letting herself be trimmed and trotted out like a poodle in any Old Folks Home either. If the worst came to the worst I'd simply have to pour all her home remedies and eau de cologne down the drain.

Gran

It must have had something to do with that letter, I'm not a fool, the way Iris was squinting and hinting about Old Folks Homes again, and dolling herself up with padded bras and swivelling her hips like a belly dancer, slapping her gender like a wet fish in everybody's face, it was pathetic. But I didn't have time to dwell on it much just then because I met Esmé McKechnie on the stairs and she said to me:

'Do you want to tell me Emily's having a baby when she's been flooding all morning?'

I said I didn't want to tell her anything. I knew a bit about herbs and remedies and things which is nature's way and often the best, but I wasn't about to call myself a gynaecologist.

'Well, I had to send her home, it was that bad,' Esmé said.

We were all pretty annoyed with Emily, there's no denying that, but we had to admit that she was a good char as chars go, which wasn't saying much, but she never had a long face when you told her to do something that she should have done weeks ago, she didn't pinch anything more than a bit of sugar or tea and she was generally on time. So we all agreed that she had got to go to the clinic like we told her in the first place. Mrs Merriman's husband sometimes left her the car, so the very next time he did she took Emily herself to make sure she got there this time, and she waited to make sure she stayed there and got herself examined by a proper white doctor even if he was only working in a clinic.

We were all waiting to hear the worst when they arrived back and we could see from Emily's face that it must be pretty bad, because she was all grey which is the palest they can go.

'She's not having a baby,' Mrs Merriman said.

Well, I could have told *her* that. You can't be having a baby and be flooding at the same time because that's a miscarriage.

'She's got lumps and tumours, but probably only fibrous tumours.'

I wasn't surprised. I'd never thought that doctor she'd gone to in South End would have known a lump from a baby.

'If it's any *other* kind of lump,' Esmé said, with a little too much relish, I thought, 'they've got this new cobalt treatment.'

'*And* they can always operate,' I said.

At that Emily began to howl, the silly gel, and we told her to shut up, we were only trying to help her.

'That's what they're *going* to do,' Mrs Merriman said. 'I spoke to the doctor myself. She's got to have a hysterectomy.'

Well, we could understand why Emily was so upset. She'd wanted a baby so badly and it was enough to upset anyone, being told that your baby is only a lump and has got to be taken out.

So to make her feel better I told her: 'Just be thankful that that lump probably isn't something even worse, because then you'll know all about it.'

But Emily went right on howling about her insides having to come out and who would marry her now because she would never have a baby and the doctor said no injections would help nor would any green medicine.

We told her to shut up again. Of course green medicine wouldn't help if she'd got to have an operation, and then the ungrateful gel said she wasn't going to have any operation.

We got a bit impatient then and told her she wasn't to think she could waste the busy doctor's time, because one never knew with lumps and anyhow she couldn't go on like that, with a pain in her back and spending all her time in the lav when we were having to pay her, and then she said she would have to talk to her sister-in-law.

'What's your sister-in-law got to do with it?' we wanted to know, but she just clammed up after that like they clam up when they get obstinate and you know that nothing is ever going to make them change their minds.

Mother

Gran was in the middle of a long story about Emily's baby that turned out to be a lump and how even she would have known the difference and I was about to ask her just how, when Girlie asked her instead, and a lot of other questions about babies too, just as if I'd never told her the facts of life and I was wondering why she should be so interested in Emily's baby that wasn't even a baby when the phone rang and I must have jumped a foot.

'Now who can that be?' I said and my voice was a bit high because it was just possible: he *could* have got my real name from the newspaper. So I patted my hair and smoothed my skirt down and it was quite a thing, getting just the right inflection in my voice when I said hello: cool, a little distant and above all, *even*. And then I said hello again, not quite so carefully this time because all I could hear was heavy breathing. And there was something unmistakable about that breathing. Only one person I knew could breathe like that.

'Phoebe?' I asked.

'Iris,' she accused. 'You never get in touch with me any more.'

'Well, I have tried,' I told her.

'Tried?' She sounded so surprised and innocent that I thought: either she's crazy or I am.

'I *phoned* you,' I said. 'And you didn't answer. All you did was breathe.'

'You didn't say who you were,' she said.

'But how did I know it was you I'd got hold of?' I asked. 'It's creepy, you know Phoebe, when someone just stands and breathes like that.'

'I *told* you,' she said. 'Odd people have been phoning me.'

'And you've disconnected your doorbell,' I reminded her. 'I knocked and knocked but you didn't answer and I could hear you moving around inside. It's creepy, you know, listening to someone moving around inside and not answering.'

'I don't open the door any more,' she said.

I had to struggle not to get my even temper ruffled. 'Well then *how* am I supposed to get in touch with you?' I asked her.

'Anyone who wants to see me can leave a note under the door or in the letter box,' she said. 'Then I'll know who it is.'

'Oh,' I said, and I thought, bugger that.

'They call me the mystery woman,' she simpered.

'Really,' I said, and I thought: she's gone crazy. Poor old Phoebe's bonkers.

'I can't take any chances,' she whispered. 'Shall I be seeing you then?'

'Sometime maybe,' I said and I put the phone down

because her whispering was giving me the creeps worse than her breathing.

'Of course,' Gran said as soon as I'd sat down again, 'she doesn't realise how lucky she is.'

'Who?' I asked. 'Phoebe?'

'*Emily*,' Gran said. 'That it's a *lump* and not a *baby*. You can't trust these tribal customs. How can she be so sure he will marry her? And then she'll be stuck with a baby and no husband. It's better to have a lump than a baby if you haven't got a husband, isn't it?'

'I'd rather have neither,' I said and I got up to make some tea. Girlie had suddenly lost interest too, I noticed, but then Gran did tend to go on and on and repeat herself ad nauseam.

Girlie

I could barely fasten my bra. I had it in the last hole but it still cut into my back and under my arms. Gran and Mother didn't notice, not even when we *talked* about babies, like Emily's, which turned out to be not a baby after all. I was sorry about that but Gran wasn't, she said she'd lived with these people longer than any of us and she knew them and if Emily had a baby, especially if she wasn't married it would only be born to suffer, and I thought maybe she was right, not about the marriage part, but the other, because I remembered what Vern had told me about that place he saw when he went off the road one day and into the veld because it was covered with flowers, millions of them, ericas and wild cosmos and proteas as big as punch bowls. But they dwindled and disappeared, even the grass disappeared, until there was only grey earth, tamped down hard and bare as stone. There were shacks and a fence and people came out, crowding up against it, to stare at him. He stared back, he said, fascinated, the way a wound fascinates you even when it's making your stomach turn.

Because they all looked so ancient, he said. Even the children looked wrinkled and ancient, old and grey and dry as the tamped-down ground they stood on.

They said there was no work and no wood for their fires and their cardboard and packing crate houses let the wind and the rain in.

They were squatters, Vern said, illegal entrants and unproductive units. With no work and not enough food they were having to drink hot water to fill themselves up when they felt hollow with hunger.

Vern said on the way back to the road the ericas were still beautiful but he wondered how much that would matter if he were as hopeless as those people were. And I thought maybe Gran was right, that it *would* be better for Emily to have a lump instead of a baby because a lump couldn't suffer, and I was going to tell her that, about what Vern had seen, so I started:

'Gran,' I said, 'you know how beautiful wild flowers are?'

'No,' she said. 'Wild flowers are full of insects and they smell awful.'

9

Mother

Weeks had gone by before I could bring myself to face the fact that he wasn't going to reply. I shouldn't have been surprised, an executive like that, with horn-rims and two telephones. But still I'd gone on for weeks, hoping like a fool. I even asked Gran once or twice if there hadn't been a letter for me.

I had kept the rough copy of my answer to his letter and I spent hours analysing it, to see where I could have gone wrong. Maybe I shouldn't have said anything about my dependants in the first letter; but I'd gone to a lot of trouble to convey that the position was bound to change, in the very nature of things. Of course I hadn't been able to say that Girlie had a special boyfriend, but I did say that she *had* had one, and it could have been that, maybe he was old-fashioned, maybe he didn't think a girl of eighteen should have a special boyfriend. Perhaps it sounded as though I wanted to get rid of them, my dependants, or was hoping to, as soon as possible. Perhaps he thought I was unkind or impatient with them which may have made him doubt that I had an even temper. Then again, it could have been the photograph I'd sent, the best one, after four tries. Maybe he hadn't really meant it when he said that beauty did not matter.

I wanted to write again, to put things right, to tell the simple truth:

Maybe I do get mad at them sometimes, who wouldn't? But I do love them. I've made a home for them, both of them, all on my own, with no help or support from anyone and sometimes I get tired and depressed, but I've made a home and I've kept it going, so if I looked old and tired in the photograph, I was tired and I could look younger, a whole lot younger, if I had just one last chance at a life of my own ...

But that sounded abject and self-pitying. The trouble was that I *was* abject and self-pitying because I'd set my heart on him, that man with his two telephones and managerial position. I knew it wouldn't do to write again, I knew I had to forget him and his square jaw and his beachfront flat and I did try but my legs went limp the evening Gran pulled a letter out of her apron pocket and waved it at me.

'Here it is,' she said, 'what you've been grousing and grumping for.'

But it wasn't. I knew that as soon as I looked at it. It wasn't his handwriting and I was so disappointed that I actually resented this stranger who was writing to me now.

I took it to the bedroom anyway, to get away from Gran because in the state I was in I wouldn't have been able to control myself if it turned out to be irregular, and from the handwriting which was undeveloped and sloped in all directions, I didn't hope for much in the way of regularity and I was right, as I realised before I'd got even halfway through it:

We were getting along very nicely with our own little house near the factory and my old Buick that I service myself over the weekends because I like to make adjustments here and there to keep it in working order like, but then I must have done something because I couldn't get it going again after the adjustments and they said at the garage it needs a full overhaul, engine out and everything, well, I haven't got a block and tackle myself so I had to send it to the garage so I got a lift with a pal and every morning and evening in the car he had these girls. Now for a while it just went in one ear and out the other, but they took so long to get the old Buick going, getting parts from here there and everywhere because they don't make them any more and I was always brought up to be grateful and things like that, because I owed him something, you know, for all the lifts I was getting, so I began to go with him and the girls until my wife got to hear about it and now she is my ex-wife. Your advert said you have two temporary dependants and my pal said that must mean you have got two children. Now I don't mind about that because I have got six myself that must come to me for the holidays. Now the old Buick has packed up for good that is why I am really looking for a lady friend with a car and a good job because I must still support all the children ...

Girlie came wandering in just then but I was too screwed-up to care. I tore the whole thing up, envelope and all and burnt the pieces in the ashtray.

'What's worth getting so hassled over?' she asked.

'*Something*,' I told her. 'What would you know? *Something's* worth getting hassled over. Something *must* be. If nothing's worth getting hassled over we might as well be *dead*.' And I started to cry.

'Okay, but cool it, Mother,' she said. 'Don't *cry*.'

I didn't expect her to understand. She'd never had anything to get hassled over, unless you counted that boy with the bell and at her age that was hardly worth counting.

And then I started thinking, all this crying. Bouts of weeping. Maybe I did have flat neurosis, but if I did, what could I do about it? I didn't have the money to pay a psychiatrist to tell me to get out of a flat that I didn't have the money to get out of.

I got up to blow my nose and saw that my nostrils were not only flaring like an old cart horse's, they were red as well, and when I put powder on them they turned purple.

But it would be all right, I told myself. It had to be. I was doing the best I could, *all* I could, trying to find someone to help me get out of that bricked-in flat, even if it was only sometimes, with a view to weekend outings, all expenses shared ...

Gran

Iris was so wrapped up in herself, moping about the place and drinking gin as if it was ginger beer that I had to tell her everything three times over and even then it didn't sink in, so I told her again:

'Emily's getting pretty useless.'

'Is that something new?' she asks.

'I don't mean useless like they get useless when they're not much use any more,' I told her. 'I mean she's not well. She's got to have this operation.'

Iris looks at me as if this is the first time she's ever heard of it, but then she can't think further than herself these days.

'Growths,' I said. 'I *told* you.'

'Oh yes, shame,' Iris says.

'Now the thing is,' I said, 'are we going to get someone in her place while she's gone? Or what?'

'Whatever you like,' Iris says as if we weren't talking about money and I could see she was losing interest. Sometimes she behaves just like a man when she comes in from work. She loses interest.

'The thing is,' I said, 'we'll have to pay her while she's away because it's not her fault and I don't think we can pay someone else as well which means paying twice, so maybe I'd better try to manage.'

'Just as you like,' Iris says, offhand, as if I wasn't trying to save her some money. 'We'll help. It can't be for long.'

'Three weeks,' I told her. 'Three weeks is plenty long enough when you're my age. And then it could be longer. You never know with growths.'

'Well, as you like,' Iris says, and she puts the newspaper up between us just like a man.

I decided I'd better keep more of an eye on Iris in future, but first the business with Emily had to be settled, so when she came in on the Friday and started limping around I asked her what her sister-in-law had to say, whatever that had got to do with it, but you never know what goes on in their minds, and she said her sister-in-law had five children and she wasn't very happy.

'Well, I'm sorry she's not very happy,' I said, 'but what has that got to do with it?'

Her sister-in-law had so many mouths to feed, Emily said, and she had to look after them.

'I'm glad about that,' I said, 'that she's looking after her children, so many don't. But what has that got to do with it?' and I could feel myself beginning to lose my patience.

'The old Madam doesn't *understand*,' Emily said and blow me if it didn't sound as if she was losing *her* patience. 'If I don't get the operation then maybe I will *die*.'

I said of course I understood that, did she think I was stupid? And she didn't answer like they don't when they know they're going to say something that you're not going to like, and I was just beginning to get really impatient when she said:

'But if I *get* the operation then how can I be a woman?'

I said 'Shame,' and I meant it because they're also human. 'But what else can you do?' I asked her.

She thought for a bit and then she said:

'I will write to my mother in East London.'

'Write to your mother in East London?' I said, and I could feel myself beginning to lose my patience again.

'I will write to my mother,' she said, 'and I will tell her about my troubles.'

'Well, perhaps you'd better tell her,' I said, 'but you better get a move on too because you can't wait too long with things like growths.'

'Someone will come from East London to look after me,' she said, 'because of my sister-in-law.'

'Because of your sister-in-law?' I asked her, because I decided then that I was going to get to the bottom of the business with her sister-in-law even if it took us the whole morning.

'Because my sister-in-law is not too happy,' she went on.

'Yes,' I said. 'So you said. But it's *your* insides, not your sister-in- law's, so what has she got to do with it?'

'Yes, old Madam,' she said very patiently, 'but my sister-in-law has got too many children so she's not too happy to look after me also.'

'Oh,' I said, because I understood it at last, which just goes to show that a little bit of patience will work wonders with these people.

'All right,' I told her, 'but you'd better hurry up and write to East London because you can't wait with these things, and what am I going to do with you now?' because she had started to hobble around again, so I gave her some of my mixture of chloric ether, tincture of ginger and sal volatile that I keep on hand in case somebody has a heart attack and we haven't got any medicinal brandy, which I know we won't have because Iris only buys gin.

Girlie

I got the book out of the library again and although I explained: 'For Physiology,' the librarian looked at me as if she knew I couldn't fasten my bra strap any more.

It was the fourth month, the time for miscarriages if you were going to have one, but I knew I wasn't.

He could frown now, the book said, but he wouldn't be; his forehead would be smooth like Vern's without a line of worry or annoyance ever. He even had vocal cords now and one day his voice would be like Vern's, slow and soft, almost singing his words, because everything Vern said had sounded like a mantra and even when I didn't really understand what he was saying I got the meaning, not with my head, but through my skin, like one understands the warmth of the sun without knowing about burning gases, or the rain on one's face without knowing about condensation and evaporation.

It was the start of the growth period and Vern would have liked that. He would have held me to him to get as close as possible to both of us.

Only he wasn't there and I felt so desolate that I had to compose myself, right there on the bathroom floor, by trying to comprehend samsara and nirvana which were One. And for a while I really felt it, that time *was* eternity; time had been an eternity ever since Vern had gone. But of course that wasn't right, that wasn't what it meant. I knew it, and I felt desolate all over again.

Mother

I put another advert in, just for laughs this time, I told myself, and I gave the office box number because I was sick and tired of Gran and Mrs McKechnie nosing in on my letters every time they came, but it didn't make much difference. The replies were all the same. Irregular. Except one, and maybe that was only because it gave nothing away.

It was almost a business letter, it actually started: re your advert. Then, could we meet and get to know each other? And a phone number. Nothing kooky at all, just straightforward and normal. This is what it's all about, I told myself, the advert and everything. We could meet, chat, and if we didn't hit it off, nobody had lost anything.

I waited until the lunch hour and then I noticed that it was a city number and I thought, wouldn't he be out for lunch? That gave me some courage, and I dialled. I knew exactly what I was going to say and even if he was in he couldn't see my sweating palms.

When the phone rang and rang and no one answered I wanted him to be in after all because I realised if he wasn't I'd have to wait the whole afternoon as well, like I'd waited the whole morning until everyone had gone because I wouldn't be able to phone from the flat, not with Gran and Girlie listening in. And then there was a click, a pause and a tentative hello. So tentative that it gave me some courage and I said brightly:

'Hello, is that... uh... White Knight?'

'Uh ... Hazel Eyes?' he asked.

'Iris,' I said, and he said: 'Sydney,' and I said:

'About meeting ...'

'Anywhere,' he said. 'Any time, you name it.'

'After work?' I said. 'Five o'clock?' because then I needn't go home and have to explain to Gran that I was going out again, and who with. I could phone and say I was working late. 'I'm in the SMA Building,' I told him. 'Shall I meet you outside?'

'Right outside,' he said. 'A green Peugeot. You can't miss it.'

I worked like a slave all that afternoon but that didn't stop the butterflies, and when five o'clock came I wanted the whole afternoon over again, but it was too late, I had to go out, and he was waiting there, in the green Peugeot, just like he'd said.

He leaned over to open the door for me and it seemed perfectly ordinary, perfectly natural, and he looked perfectly ordinary and natural, a bit hairy perhaps, but he didn't stare at me or anything embarrassing like that, and I relaxed a little.

'Where to?' he asked. 'A drink? Coffee?'

I needed a drink badly but to play it safe I said: 'Coffee, if that's okay. But if you'd rather have a drink that's okay too; I mean, I'm not a teetotaller, or any thing like that, so if you ...' and I stopped because I was practically gabbling.

He smiled at me, a nice, decent, ordinary smile and said: 'I don't mind telling you, I was relieved when I saw you. One doesn't know, I mean, the sort of people ... I was a bit nervous myself, before I saw you.'

'I know,' I said. 'It isn't easy, especially if you're a woman.'

'It isn't easy if you're a man either,' he said.

I began to feel good, better than I've felt for a long time and over coffee we talked, mainly about Gran and Girlie because he was so interested. I told him that Girlie seemed to be putting on puppy fat all over again and he said she sounded sweet. He said he thought I was wonderful, caring for Gran too, because so many people didn't bother about their parents these days and a home wasn't a home without a sweet little old Grannie sitting by the fire. I didn't see Gran quite like that so I thought I'd better prepare him:

'Actually, Gran's still very energetic,' I said, and he said wonderful, wonderful, at her age.

I was feeling so confident by then that I even told him that Girlie had one or two odd ideas, and he said wonderful, wonderful, young people should think for themselves. I said yes, but meditations and gurus and things? And he said wonderful, wonderful, he'd read all about it, but wasn't it time we got out of that smoky place?

We only drove as far as the harbour because I said I mustn't be home too late and he parked right at the end, behind the sheds.

'Meeting someone like you is like coming home,' he said, which was so nice that I started telling him more about Gran and Girlie in my lightest, most humorous vein, until I noticed that he'd got his fly open and before I could do anything like push him away or get out of the car it was over. He had come all over me, just like that, over my lap and my legs and my hands.

I was actually heaving as I struggled with the door handle.

'What's wrong with you?' he kept asking. 'You've been married before. Christ, it's not as if you're a bloody virgin, what do you think it's all about?' and when I'd got out and started running he called after me:

'And your eyes aren't even hazel, they're plain bloody brown!'

I didn't stop to ask him: and what sort of a White Knight are you? I just ran, cleaning myself up with tissues as best I could, and on the bus back home I tried to be philosophical about it, telling myself that I was lucky, that he could have been another sort of maniac, he could have tried to murder me.

73

But I didn't feel lucky at all, I felt terrible, and I felt even worse when I saw Gran and Girlie, and for a long time afterwards I told myself, never again, not ever again.

10

Gran

Girlie ate as though she had a mechanical jaw and she was getting nice and plump off it too, but lately Iris was picking about at her food until I couldn't stand it any more.

'Is something wrong?' I asked her. 'Are you on a diet again?'

She looked at me as though she'd been waiting for me to say that. 'It's this,' she said, 'and it isn't even all that cold.'

'What isn't even all that cold?' I asked her. 'You're as bad as Emily. No getting any sense out of either of you.'

'It isn't even all that cold but we're having to eat stew every night,' Iris says. 'You even stewed that chicken I brought home to roast.'

I could see we were in for it the way she said it and my blood pressure gave a little surge. It does one good to clear the air every once in a while because Iris is altogether too wrapped up in herself these days, so I said:

'You may not know it, Iris, but there's an art to feeding old folk. They need more balanced feeding. And that's the latest findings.'

'And what's so balanced about stew?' she asks.

'Just let me finish,' I told her. 'How can I tell you anything if you never let me finish?'

Iris rolls her eyes up and I thought yes, that's given you something to think about outside of yourself.

'Well finish,' she says. 'What about it?'

'The latest findings,' I told her, 'are that elderly people need food that can be easily chewed and digested. And stews are the best because they are the easiest to chew and digest and they encourage the eating of vegetables because the long cooking has made them soft.'

'So from now on we're going to get nothing but stew?' Iris asks. 'You're even going to stew chicken?'

Her voice was getting higher and higher but I ignored the tone of it because it was always so unnecessary, even for clearing the air. 'And the most satisfactory puddings are made with milk,' I told her, to give her something else to think about.

Iris banged her knife and fork down which is also unnecessary and asked: 'Now do you want me to buy more milk?'

'You'll please yourself Iris, as usual,' I said. 'I'm just telling you about the nutritional requirements of old folks, that's all. It's all right when you're young, you can eat any old thing without getting indigestion, the only thing is that in the days when I could eat any old thing there was never anything to eat, going through the Depression like we did, just when my bones were forming and my teeth, no wonder they went all soft, I never really had strong teeth like other people, I never had any calcium to speak of, that's why I was always at the dentist's, if you remember. Soft enamel, he said, and no wonder.'

'Not while we're trying to eat,' Iris says, 'for God's sake.'

'*What* not while we're trying to eat?' I asked her. I swear I'm not making much sense of Iris these days, which makes it a real job of work, arguing with her.

'Talking about teeth,' she says.

'And what's wrong with teeth?' I asked her. 'You had good hard enamel and nice strong bones, never had you to a dentist I didn't, and you should be thanking God for that, instead of taking His name in vain every end and side.'

'Enamel?' Iris snorts. She's my own daughter but I must say she sounds just like a horse sometimes. 'I started losing my teeth before I was thirty!'

'That's not bad going,' I told her. 'You can thank the maizena or calzana or whatever it was that I gave you for that. It was full of calcium and there isn't anything wrong with your bones as far as I can see.'

'Could I have some more?' Girlie said then and we both turned to look at her.

'Hadn't you better be watching your weight?' Iris asks her.

'Leave her alone,' I said. 'It's a good stew, you don't want her looking like that model gel what's-her-name, Sticky, while they're starving in India and China, or we'll be having to pay for it later with brittle bones and crumbling teeth when it's too late. What good's it doing me now, a stew like this when it's too late to feed my bones and my teeth are plastic already?'

'Plastic?' Iris snorts, better than any horse.

'Well, whatever they are,' I said. 'The point is that no matter what I eat now, no matter how many milk puddings and things like that it's too late to put enamel on because there's nothing left to put enamel on to.'

Iris got up to clear the table. 'Don't make me laugh, Gran,' she says, 'God knows I feel more like crying.'

'And I'm not surprised,' I told her, 'taking the Lord's name in vain, blaspheming all over the place, God this, God that and God the other, it's enough to make one's hair stand on end, gives me the cold shivers, it does, aren't you afraid that a bolt of lightning'll come right down and strike you dead?'

'Well, what have I got to lose,' she asks, 'if I've got to live on the nutritional requirements of old folks before my time?'

It was the way she said it that made me laugh, and I could feel that the air was a whole lot clearer, like it hasn't been ever since that night she was supposed to be working late.

'Well, if you're going to make such a song and dance about it,' I told her, 'I'll do you roast chicken every now and then, with a bit of stew on the side for myself.'

Then again, when I came to think about it, I thought, a small peck of roast chicken every now and then wouldn't do me much harm either, seeing I'd already lost my enamel, as long as I made a good thick milk pudding to go along with it.

Girlie

I'd gained about ten pounds, I could see it and I could feel it
and I tried to stop eating but I was so hungry all the time that
I couldn't. Mother and Gran had noticed, and I had the feeling
outside too, with strangers in the street, that they knew, and I
didn't want to go out any more, so I said I wasn't feeling well,
but Gran said nonsense, all I needed was some sunshine and
fresh air, I was only 'fleshing out' nicely, which made me feel
like a sheep being fattened for the slaughter, only I looked
more like a cow with my bust so big and droopy that I sweated
underneath.

My stomach was getting bigger too, and I was afraid they'd
notice that as well, so I sat with my arms folded over it, but
sitting forward like that made my bust look even bigger and
they were on at me all the time about bad posture and giving
myself an ugly round back and shoulders.

I didn't want to have to say anything about the baby any
more. It would be too impossible. I thought I'd just leave it
until there was no *need* to say anything, except that I couldn't
go back to lectures. I didn't even want to go out pretending
that I was going. I thought of putting a loose dress on and
sitting in the park; I thought of disappearing, of trying to find
Vern, but I couldn't just start walking and maybe have the
baby on the roadside.

I must have panicked a bit because I felt I just had to talk
to them, to Mother or Gran, only I couldn't *plan* anything, I
couldn't plan what I was going to say, if I had I wouldn't have
been able to say anything, so in the end all I said was: 'Mother,
I can't go back to lectures,' and I hung my head because that's
what she would have expected me to do.

And she said: 'What do you mean? What are you talking
about?' her voice already going up, getting ready to say I
needn't even think about it at my age, about going to work
because I was going to finish at the university which was
what everyone was sacrificing for and which was more than

she'd ever had a chance to do, all of which I knew off by heart already so before she could get started I said:

'I'm getting fat, Mother, my stomach is showing,' and I felt an awful coward, angling in on it like that.

She stared at me, looking puzzled, and then more puzzled and then so wildly puzzled that her eyes grew big and I knew that she knew what I was trying to say and I knew that she didn't want to know. I thought: of course she's seen, she *must* have seen, how couldn't she have seen, even though I always dressed and undressed with my back to her? But of course she wouldn't *want* to see, she wouldn't *want* to know, although she must have seen by now.

She spoke very carefully and lightly in an awful false sort of way. 'You *have* been putting on weight. It's all those stews Gran's been giving us. She thickens the gravy with flour. I'm putting on weight too. Only mine's middle-age spread. It's all that starch.'

'It isn't *only* the starch, Mother,' I said, because I had to put an end to it. But she didn't want to know.

'Look, don't be silly,' she said. 'We'll go on diet. It's easier when two people are dieting together. They can watch each other and make a bit of a competition of it. Only I know who'll win. At your age it'll just melt off you!' and she laughed, an awful false sort of laugh which made me feel even worse. So bad in fact that I put my arms around her and began to cry, because I could see how much it was going to hurt her, when she would *have* to face it.

She patted my back in a distracted way and said: 'Shush, shush. Don't let Gran hear you. If you carry on like this Gran'll be in here in a minute.'

'Mother, I'm sorry,' I said, because I could see how it was going to be for her and I was dreadfully sorry, but she suddenly went all sharp and fierce.

'Nonsense,' she said. 'You've got nothing to be sorry for. I don't know what you're talking about.'

But I could see that she did know and I just couldn't say

anything more. I'd have to wait until she stopped pretending that she didn't know, that it wasn't the truth. In the meantime I'd have to go on going to lectures. Just for a few more days, I told myself, and I'd wear my loosest dresses, which helped a bit, but that didn't stop me from feeling all full and bloated and scared inside.

Gran

There's no pleasing Iris or Girlie these days, heaven knows. I did them roast after roast and never mind the cost, not that they didn't eat them, especially Girlie.

I think a girl should be well covered myself, I never did care for this new fashion of looking like a cow in a drought but everything in moderation, I always say, because she's beginning to look a bit like a balloon, the way she's swelling out and I had to tell her, people are going to think you're expecting.

Then Iris goes off pop and tells me not to say things like that, and what am I trying to do? I ask you! Girlie knows the facts of life by now and it was only us, no men or anything present, so why is everyone so touchy these days, I wondered, what's so terrible about a little joke like that?

And it isn't as though Iris is exactly the soul of modesty herself, drinking gin like water and writing to strange men in the papers. I was that piqued I didn't even say it's an ill wind, and at least Girlie was having to wear nice little frocks these days instead of her everlasting jeans.

But Iris hasn't been herself lately. In fact she hasn't been herself for some time and I've never pretended to understand all her moods and manners. Where she gets them from heaven only knows, not from me at any rate, or her late father. He had his faults but he wasn't a moody man, although that was more than you could say for his mother and you never can tell who is going to take after who. Moods and things can to be inherited and you can't always be blaming the poor parents either, not when they've got mothers-in-law like I had, but there you are.

So there I had the pair of them on my hands and no pleasing either of them. Girlie was walking around as though the world was about to come to an end and Iris was walking around with a besotted look in her eyes like the world *had* come to an end.

There was no making sense of either of them, and I had worries enough of my own, like I told Esmé McKechnie on the stairs. Nothing about Iris or Girlie, mind. There's no sense in putting gossip into people's mouths, especially Esmé's, so we just talked about Emily and all the inconvenience she was putting us to and I just had to tell her what Emily had said to me, it was so funny.

'You know, old Madam,' she said, 'I think you are right when you say it can be ancer because it feels just like ancer.'

I might have known that Esmé wouldn't catch on.

'Answer?' she says, 'it feels like answer?'

'*Can*cer,' I told her. 'She meant *can*cer.' And I couldn't even be bothered to ask her how she thought Emily thought she knew what cancer feels like, although that was the whole point of the story.

'Mmmmm,' Esmé said, as though she'd caught on in the first place, 'so what's she doing about it?'

'The latest,' I said, 'is that her mother can't send anyone down here to look after her so she's going home to have it done there so that her mother can look after her.'

'Home?' Esmé said. 'To East London? But that's going to take up more time, the travelling and all that.'

'Well, at least we know now,' I said. 'We know where we stand.' I don't know about other people but I always like to know where I stand so that I can plan things accordingly. 'Her mother lives in Duncan Village and she's going to the Frere Hospital.'

Esmé passed the word on; you can always count on her for that, and we all paid Emily and wished her good luck, and told her she had to be back in three weeks' time and we were all holding thumbs for her and Mrs Goedhals gave her two old warm nighties for the hospital and Iris gave her the bedjacket I knitted for her when she was expecting Girlie. As good as new it was, but then they don't make wool like that any more, not that I could knit so fine any more either.

Mrs Merriman even took her down to the station so she wouldn't have to carry her suitcase from the bus stop and it just made me so mad, thinking what they're always saying about us overseas when we let Emily go like that and helped her on her way because she was so much happier about going to her mother to have the operation there.

But I didn't fancy not knowing what was going on for three whole weeks and you can never trust these people to write so I gave Emily a stamped, addressed envelope to give to the doctor so that he could write and tell us how it was all going off.

Emily promised to write too, so it was all settled at last. It wouldn't be easy managing without her because she did at least know where we kept everything, but of course there was no point in hanging on, not with lumps and growths and things. So that was one weight off my mind.

11

Mother

I'd had enough of the whole sorry business, but it was surprising how many kooks and cranks were still answering the last advert I'd put in. I wondered when it was going to stop, but I read them all; I had to see just how weird they could get, like *Small Package*:

> *I think the trouble was that we got married late in life, after being free for so long. My ex-wife was 42 and I was 45, but I think I adjusted better than she did. If I hadn't been able to give, give, give … I think we stuck it out for so long because of the sex side. I'm a tremendous lover, I don't mind warning you. You wouldn't think it to look at me, but good things come in small packages. Anyway, that side of it was a bit of all right maybe because we'd never had it before. But I'd been a bachelor for so long that I was too well organised and the breaking point came when she cleaned my pantry out and threw away the hairpin I use for testing my pastry. I nearly sjambokked her, I don't mind telling you, and we broke up over it. But now I miss the sex part. I don't mind telling you straight, I don't really want to get married again. I don't want another woman interfering with my hairpins, but if you're interested in some really tremendous sex …?*

That was the way they went, some a bit better, some a whole lot worse, and amongst them all only one that was more or less reasonable, or at least not too irregular. And that was *Shrunken Head*.

> *In the end I went to a psychiatrist*, he wrote, *and he looked a bit like a rabbit. Come to think of it, the whole business was Wonderlandish. 'I've got this terrific resentment against my wife,'*

I told him: 'We've all got resentments,' he said. 'I'm worried sick,' I told him. 'We all are,' he said. That was all the help he could give me, but luckily I have now found the answer: True Enlightenment, which I want to share with everybody. It's a whole new way of life. Without it I'm convinced that only the worst can happen to one.

I reread that several times, trying to get some idea of what he meant, and I became more and more intrigued, wondering what the resentment was and the new way of life that he wanted to share. One thing I was certain of, and that was if nothing happened to get me out of the rut I was in, the worst was going to happen to me. There was a word for *Shrunken Head*'s letter and it took me a long time to think of it. It was on the tip of my tongue for days and then at last I got it: cryptic. He didn't say anything much. He didn't ask about my dependants, if any. He didn't even want a photograph. I became really curious but I couldn't bring myself to do anything about it because of what had happened with White Knight. I just couldn't take another chance, until the night Phoebe phoned.

I knew it would be Phoebe even before I heard the heavy breathing which practically misted up my earhole.

So I said: 'Phoebe.'

'You never did contact me,' she said, all bitter and accusing, after a long breathy pause.

'I've been busy,' I said, 'and all that business, you know, leaving notes under your door and …'

'That was only a little misunderstanding,' she said.

'Misunderstanding?' I didn't understand. 'You mean you *don't* want me to leave notes under your door?'

'Do you want to know something,' she said, and she dropped down to a whisper that I could hardly hear over her breathing. 'The other day Mrs Radomsky came down, or perhaps it was Mrs Rabbalini, and gave me a red carnation, just a single red carnation.'

'What for?' I asked, and I thought: poor old Phoebe.

'I keep her butter in my fridge,' Phoebe said. 'She hasn't got a fridge.'

'Oh,' I said.

'And when are you going to come around?' she asked.

I hesitated, because I didn't feel I could take Phoebe just then, but before I could say anything she was screaming that she knew I was never going to come, and didn't I know she'd keep my butter in her fridge for me with pleasure?

'I've got my own fridge,' I said.

'Oh,' she screamed. 'Now I know why people commit suicide!' and she banged the phone down.

I suspected she was only trying to frighten me but I wondered whether I hadn't better contact Suicides Anonymous on her behalf, only I didn't want to make a fool of myself, saying that I thought my friend was going to commit suicide because there was no need for her to keep my butter in her fridge, so I phoned her instead and after a long time she answered, or at least I heard heavy breathing, so she must have been all right.

I wasn't, though. I was dead scared. I could see myself ending up like Phoebe with nothing in my life but a single red carnation and maybe not even that, which I suppose was the worst that could happen, so I made up my mind to take another chance, just one last chance.

Shrunken Head probably had a kooky reason for resenting his wife. There was probably something wrong with her nose. She probably ate too much or drank too much or needed false teeth, or interfered with his hairpins. There was bound to be something weird somewhere. On the other hand, he did sound quite well educated. At least he had heard of *Alice in Wonderland*. And God knew I could do with a bit of enlightenment. So I wrote. But I gave the office phone number, because if Gran answered the phone and someone said: 'This is Shrunken Head,' she'd call the police.

Girlie

It was a real sweat, trying not to get hassled. It would have helped if I'd been able to achieve one-pointedness, but that was a sweat too, reciting a mantra and fixing my attention on the smoke coming out of the power station chimney because that was all I could see from my bed and it was pretty hopeless. Dirty black smoke isn't like a green field or a garden of flowers with some living beauty you can lose yourself in. There wasn't the tiniest bit of blue sky, only black smoke, and trying to pierce through that, even with my mind, made me feel like coughing.

I hadn't got very far with yama either because I just couldn't extinguish all desires or at least the only real desire I'd ever had and I couldn't try to extinguish it without thinking about what I was trying to extinguish, and that would bring it all back, so real that it took my breath, literally, because I could actually *feel* him again, and that fantastic throb that came down, pulsing right on up inside me.

Vern always said I was a sensualist, that I wanted everything full and profuse. He said I was like a thick, matted, dark green forest with secret shadows where everything was lush, and he told me about the forests down the sides of the Long Tom Pass where the pine needles felt like foam-rubber under one's feet. A foam-rubber forest, he said, soft and resilient, smelling fresh and green even when the pines were vague and smoky in the mist of an early morning.

I realised that I wasn't even seeing the smoke any more and I thought, if I had to fix my mind on something, couldn't it be Vern, which was so easy? But perhaps that would be idolatry, although I was only meditating, not worshipping.

I tried then to get *beyond Vern* to the *idea* of love, but it didn't exist for me without him. I knew that couldn't be right. I wasn't getting anywhere, so I tried the lotus position, and reducing all bodily movement to a minimum, even breathing, but that must have upset the baby because he started to kick me under the ribs. Maybe he wasn't getting enough oxygen in that position and I couldn't control *his* bodily movements.

I don't think yoga was meant for pregnant women. They're too distracted and examining the distractions and tracing them to their sources only led one back to the beginning, for me to the beginning on the beach with Vern and that brought all the desire flooding back again that one was supposed to extinguish before you could even begin with the concentration and the breathing or any of the rest of it.

Mother

Shrunken Head phoned about a week later but I was very wary. I made a little joke about his resentments to see if they happened to include plumpness, flaring nostrils, the odd drink, dependants or the colour of one's eyes and he laughed rather pleasantly and said:

'Oh that. I shouldn't even have mentioned it. I'm not hard to please, nobody's perfect and it's the state of one's *mind* that matters, isn't it?'

I agreed with all that, perhaps a shade too enthusiastically, so to cover up I asked him his name, and he laughed again and said:

'Ivor Novello Brown,' and I laughed too because I thought it must be a joke until he went on:

'My mother was mad keen on music, you see. I'm mad keen on music too, although not Novello of course. Tell me, are you mad keen on music?'

I said: 'Oh yes,' because I really don't mind music as long as it's got some sort of a tune to it.

'Say, that's tremendous,' he said, 'because I'm throwing a little musicale this evening, bite to eat and so on. I've got the greatest sitar. How does that grab you?'

I thought a musicale would be a lot safer than driving to the harbour wall so I said I'd love to. I didn't know what sitar was and I didn't want to show my ignorance but I assumed it must be something to eat, and although I don't generally like odd foods like oysters and snails I thought I'd give it a try, I was feeling so optimistic already.

Ivor – it didn't sound so odd without the Novello tacked on – told me the time and the place and it sounded like one of those posh blocks of bachelor flats with potted rubber trees and a modern art design in the foyer because it had a fancy Italian name which I didn't catch. Ivor said I couldn't miss it, everyone knew it and I didn't want to appear out of touch. He must have thought I had my own car because he didn't offer to pick me up, which was a relief actually because I didn't want him to meet Gran and Girlie just yet. First impressions are too important and whatever else might be said about them, they didn't look the sort of people who went to musicales. I didn't either, I suppose, but I hoped I'd be able to carry it off. I'd simply watch what the other guests did and do likewise.

I decided to take a taxi and I thought of saying that my car was in for servicing. He'd probably offer to take me home then which would be all right because Gran and Girlie would be asleep, and I could save on the fare back. Only then I'd have to say later that I'd sold the car so he wouldn't find out I'd been lying, which is always the trouble if you start lying in the first place and in any case Gran and Girlie would ask: 'What car?' sooner or later when they met him so I'd just have to think of something else.

I realised he was saying goodbye and luckily he said again: 'Don't forget now. Toledo,' or I would have spent a fortune on the taxi, driving to all the bachelor flats in town that had potted plants and modern art and Italian-sounding names. Unless of course he'd said 'toodle-de-do', but I'd have to cross that one when I came to it.

It was agony, trying to decide what to wear, what a sophisticated, mad keen music-loving woman of the world who eats exotic food would be likely to wear, because I wanted

Ivor's first impression of me to be just right. Only I didn't have anything that looked nearly sophisticated or mad keen enough so in the end I decided to dress very carelessly, as though I cared so much about music that I couldn't care less about clothes.

Gran looked a bit startled when she saw me and she sniffed like she always does when I'm going out on my own which is once in about every five years, and asked me where I thought I was going, tricked out like that.

'To listen to some good music for a change,' I told her.

'Looks more like a shipwreck dance or hobo party to me,' she said, and: 'Good music? I thought your hobby was writing letters?'

Gran has always had this knack of making me feel like a sixteen-year-old which at my age I wouldn't have minded if it didn't annoy me so much, so I said nothing.

'One of those municipal concerts, is it?' she went on probing. 'You've never gone to them before. Although I've never minded a bit of music myself. Maybe I should go along with you, do me good, to get out for a bit. And there's Girlie sitting cross-legged on her bed in a trance; all she's short of is a snake to charm. Do her good to get out for a while too.'

'It's a private concert,' I told her, 'and I can't wait now. And that's only yoga Girlie's doing, exercises for posture.'

I left Gran snorting that if it was posture Girlie was after she was going to end up with legs like a corkscrew the way she was going, but I had to run because I had to phone for a taxi from the public phone right at the end of the block so Gran wouldn't be able to tell me how much cheaper it would be, going by bus, and then I had to stand and wait in the box, pretending to be phoning until the taxi came in case someone thought I was a streetwalker, or grabbed my bag or something.

I was pretty strung up by the time I got to Ivor's flat, but at least I realised I'd done the right thing in dressing casually, because Ivor was dressed very casually indeed; either that or he hadn't finished dressing because all he had on was a pair of pants and a medallion. I thought his hair was a bit long and his eyes too close together and he squinted ever so slightly, but that wasn't his fault, not having good looks. One thing he did have was money. You could see that, from the handwoven rugs and handcarved furniture and the hi-fi that looked like the dashboard or whatever it is of an aeroplane.

I was glad I was the first to arrive so that we could get to know a bit about each other, but he didn't talk at all, he just handed me a strong orange-coloured drink and put a record on. At first I thought a flock of birds had become entangled in the electric wires outside because an extraordinary twanging and jangling filled the whole room, but when he smiled at me and nodded I realised that it was coming from the huge speakers in the corners and I wondered if it would be too obvious if I moved away from the one that was jangling in my ear and making my teeth rattle, or whether I should wait until the other guests arrived and then take up a position on the balcony or in the kitchen.

Ivor handed me another dish of the herby-tasting orange stuff and said, said: 'How does it grab you? The sitar?'

I sipped politely and said it was very nice although I thought it tasted an awful lot like the cough mixture Gran concocts and I wondered whether it would be rude to ask for gin.

We were well into our third sitar before I began to suspect that no one else was coming.

'Isn't anyone else coming?' I shouted over the fearful twanging. 'To your musicale?'

He picked up a little baton and began to beat time to the music – if that was what you could call it – on his palm. 'You can't enjoy the sitar in a crowd,' he said. 'It's an intimate experience. But let's have something to eat.'

I couldn't see what was all that intimate about it, except the way it burnt holes in one's stomach lining, but I thought something to eat would help fill them up before they became bleeding ulcers, and he just might, I hoped, turn the infernal jangling off while we ate. But he didn't. He went out and brought in bowls of what I hoped were nuts and but looked more like birdseed. I chewed a few but they got stuck under my dental plate and began to hurt like hell.

I knew I'd have to go to the bathroom to rinse my mouth out or I wouldn't be able to talk properly, so I got up, thinking no, it's not going to work. Girlie might like his long hair and bare feet and medallion but that sort of thing doesn't impress Gran much. Or me. I could maybe learn to live with the twanging and even the sitar which must be an acquired taste, as long as there were all those rugs and things to make up for it, but I do like a nice roast that doesn't feel like gravel in my mouth.

So I decided to wash my plate and say goodnight, the music was literally out of this world, when he came at me with his little baton.

I was too startled to bolt and my mouth was too full of birdseed to scream so I just stood while he beat a little tattoo right up my legs to my thighs but when he undid my skirt and started on my behind I leapt forward, my skirt dropped to my ankles and I fetched up on my knees. Before I could get up he had pulled my pants down and was whacking my bare bottom quite hard.

'I'm going to do this all over,' he said. 'Until you're glowing pink and just a little bit sore, just sore enough to be pleasurable.'

'That's what you think,' I mumbled, spraying half-chewed seeds all over his handwoven rug.

'No, no, wait and see,' he said. 'It's through the yang that one reaches the yin, you know.'

All I wanted to reach was the door and I hate to think what I must have looked like, crawling along like that with my pants around my feet and my bare bottom stuck up in the air with him whacking it and my mouth stuffed with whatever seeds they were.

I got to my feet somehow and got my pants and skirt up and the door open while he stood shaking his head with pity, I suppose, for my unenlightenment because he went on explaining that one had to pass through yang to be purged and get to yin, but all I wanted to pass through was the door.

I tore down the street to the taxi rank, trying to tidy myself up and praying that Gran and Girlie would be asleep when I got there. And I told myself it was the last time, I promised myself, so help me, no more kooks and cranks and maniacs.

No wonder he had resentments against his wife. She probably objected to having the yang beaten out of her too. I calmed down a bit in the taxi and I thought, if Gran and Girlie *were* up I'd tell them it *had* been a shipwreck party, with music, only everyone thought I didn't look shipwrecked enough. Because Gran would never understand about *Shrunken Head*, let alone all that about yin and yang. She'd say it sounded like old-fashioned irregularity to her, and the hell of it was I'd just have to agree with her.

Vern

I was beginning to free my mind from its attachment to the senses, and slowly losing even the memory of that hacking cough that had bugged me for so long, spoiling me for everything, worse even than the grubs. Only once there was a crow or something in the late afternoon and that brought it all back: Dad, big and pudgy, like his cough should have been real rich and squelchy instead of thin and dry and rattly like old chicken bones being tossed together.

I remember I'd got the idea, when I was still a kid, that the real Dad was the one the cough belonged to and the Dad everyone saw was just a wrapping, like getting a great big promising-looking present, all bound up in gold tissue and scarlet ribbons. So much wrapping that you never got to the present, but you'd go on looking, thinking it's got to be in there somewhere, because no one's ever going to take so much trouble wrapping nothing.

Except Dad, as I realised later, and Mom must have known for years.

I sat down and breathed for six to beat the memories out, held for three, Om in slowly for six from under the navel and up the vagus, held it for three, slower and slower, beating the memories and the panic and the angst and the grubs until everything was more or less flat and unruffled, the valley a smooth quilt of colour, consciousness suspended still as the hawk that hung high up there, above the macadam, disdainful of me on the roadside immobile as a meerkat on the rock, or the small nervy buck I saw just then poised like a ballet dancer against the perfectly stage-set antheaps.

Even so, it stayed with me, Dad and his cough and the big hassle we'd had because he was always on at me to state my convictions, even before I had any. I told him that 'conviction' was too strong and arrogant a word for any of the ideas I had, that all I had were intuitions and insights, fleeting and flexible as circumstances themselves.

'Life's like a flowing river, Dad,' I said, 'on the move all the time, and holding convictions is like trying to stay on your feet in midstream when the current is swirling and changing direction all around you. You go under, convictions and all, which is maybe very

93

heroic but it's also very stupid and blind and arrogant and a hell of a waste.'

That made him launch into the pitfalls awaiting those who lacked the old-fashioned virtues of ambition and direction and conviction, so I told him I was a Buddhist, lacking all those particular virtues on principle.

He looked a bit stricken then, like that thin dry cough could really belong to him.

I hadn't wanted to get on to Buddha, seeing as how Mom always said not to make trouble. But that's the way it was with Dad and me. He said if he'd laid all those good foundations to no avail it was the end, he didn't want to live under the same roof as a heathen. Mom said: 'George!' but he looked at her and she didn't say anything more. I said: 'Right on!' and I would have split right then, except Mom said: 'Don't go,' just like Girlie, so I stayed on in the toolshed until she died of a cerebral haemorrhage in the night.

Even then Dad wouldn't let it be. He had to know what I was going to do with my life.

'Split,' I told him.

'How?' he wanted to know.

'On my sandals,' I said. 'And when they wear out, on my bare feet.'

'Where to?'

I didn't know that myself yet, so I said: 'Down the road.'

And that was where I went, down the road, but it was all that hassle with Dad and Mom going like that that brought the grubs on and they spoilt me for everything for a long time, even walking, because even when my legs had begun to feel solid again they were there, burrowing up under my skin, like now, just remembering all that, even when I was under a real clear sky, looking at real sharp birds, I felt good and unnerved, like I was blocked in by concrete again, and mocked by strutting city pigeons, all bloated with sly, sinister eyes.

Sometimes I can get stoned on my breathing, my thoughts like images on a screen, projected, sliding in, sliding out, all in slow motion, but not now. Now it was Girlie's face taking over from

Dad's and Mom's. It came on and held and wouldn't slide out and all the little things came back with it, odd, inconsequential bits of conversation, like that time I'd told her about the spreeus, zillions of them, strung out along the telegraph wires. 'A colossal twittering machine,' I said, 'a living Klee.'

And she'd wanted to know: 'You mean like in feet of?' And it didn't bug me because she was like that, sharp and soft and a bit silly all at the same time, like when she'd pretended not to understand that you couldn't say a mantra for someone else.

The panic and the grubs were retreating, leaving only the inner ache, that could have been damped-down angst, or that projection of Girlie's face that wouldn't slide out.

I swung on again, out on to the road, miles and miles of it like it was never going to end, but that didn't bug me either. I fixed my mind on the very end of it, where it converged to a tiny point and concentrated on the mechanics of walking, right foot heel rising, on to the ball, left foot rising, down, heel up, on to the ball, characterising each action separately in my head and already the spasms in my legs were going and I was collecting, integrating all the fraying, wavering threads of my being preparatory to weaving them into the right, tight concentrated warp and woof necessary to unjangle my vibes, achieve the immobility, the great satisfaction, but most of all, the freedom from inner pain.

Part Two

1

Girlie

I wasn't hiding it any more, or trying to, with step-ins or anything. I thought, when they had to know, they'd know. But Mother was still pretending and she went on pretending until the day I stopped going to lectures and Gran told her I must be ill. She couldn't go on pretending then. She said:

'You *have* put on weight, haven't you? You're developing quite a little paunch, aren't you?' and I said: 'Yes, but it isn't all that little any more, is it?'

She looked at me for a long time. Finally she said: 'You know, you're really beginning to look ...' and she stood, quietly, looking at me and facing up to it for the first time and getting paler and paler. I felt really sorry for her and I would have said something, to ease it a little but she began to babble: 'You're not ... oh no, you're not ... of course not. You wouldn't. Of course not. Would you?'

I didn't say anything. I couldn't think of anything to say. I had to wait for her to get there, like she was climbing a mountain, she had to get to the top by herself and I had to wait until she got there.

'You *are!*' she said and she collapsed on the bed like she was exhausted after that climb.

I wanted to touch her. 'Mother,' I said.

She jumped up, not angry, just sort of wild with panic.

'How long?' she asked me. 'I mean, how far?'

I didn't get that, so I just looked at her.

'How far are you *gone*?' she said, in a terrible piercing whisper, because of Gran, I suppose. I didn't think of it like that, like being *gone*, but I knew what she meant, so I said: 'Five, six months,' and she said:

'Five, six months! Then it's too late. Oh, Girlie! For an

abortion.'

'But I don't want …' I said. 'Who said I want …?' and I saw all those little furry animals again, plastered all over the road, swimming in their blood.

'And I can't afford it,' she went on, 'and I don't know where to go if I could afford it.' She started wailing. 'Oh my God. Oh my *God*!' and then she collapsed on the bed again until another thought struck her, and she jumped up.

'Of course, you'll have to get married! Why didn't I think of that? It's almost too late, but it's the only thing. Where is he? Who's the father?'

I told her I didn't know where he was and she started to go wild, grabbing my arms, shaking me and hissing, so Gran wouldn't hear: 'Where is he? You're going to tell me!'

I told her again, I didn't know, and she hissed:

'It's him isn't it? That one with the long hair? You're going to tell me!'

I said I didn't know, I didn't know where he was, but she wouldn't believe me. I felt sorry for her, but I couldn't believe it was *that* terrible. It wasn't as terrible as hatred, or cruelty, or murder, or war, and I tried to tell her that but she shook me and then she pinched my arm, really hard, pulling the skin out and twisting it.

'You're going to tell me,' she said.

Tears came into my eyes and I panted with the pain.

'I don't know,' I gasped. 'Maybe he's in Kathmandu, listening to sitar …'

'*Sitar!*' she almost yelled, as though it was something real unholy, getting ready to pinch again. 'I know all about *that*!' with a crazy wild look in her eye. 'That explains it! He made you drink that stuff, beat you on the legs and bottom and then raped you! I'm getting the police!'

'No!' I said. 'He didn't beat me or make me drink anything. I never said …'

'And you're only eighteen! I'll get Interpol,' she said. 'What's his full name?'

'I don't know, honestly,' I said, because I didn't. I'd never thought of asking. Maybe his real name was Vernon. I didn't know.

'We'll give his description then,' she said. 'Long hair, beard, blue jeans, old tyres for sandals. What else?' But I could see she was beginning to give up because that description would fit everybody on the road, just about, and especially in Kathmandu.

'He could have gone to Turkey, or Tibet,' I said, 'or Nepal, or ...'

'Kathmandu is in Nepal,' she snapped, 'as you'd know if you'd paid some attention to your education instead of ... You don't *want* to find him, do you?' And she looked at me suspiciously. 'Why not? Don't you care for him at all?'

That hurt worse than the pinching and tears came into my eyes again.

'If he wants to, he'll come back,' I told her. 'I can't hunt him and run him to ground. He's got to do his own thing. I care for him that much. Maybe marriage turns him off ...'

She began banging her fists on the wall. I'd never seen her so hassled. '*I'd* like to turn him off,' she said. 'Swilling sitar in Nepal, leaving you to suffer!'

That bugged me a bit. 'I'm not suffering,' I said. 'Not like you mean anyway. And he doesn't swill it, he listens to it.'

'*Listens* to it?' she asked. 'To what? It doesn't even have bubbles!'

I didn't know what she was talking about but I didn't have a chance to find out because she started hugging and rocking me and crying into my hair that we were two of a kind, there must be something wrong with us because we only attracted the kooks and the maniacs, never mind whether they wore suits or bells, they were all crazy and we had to suffer for it, because someone who sat listening to sitar was obviously a maniac, although that was probably a lot better than drinking it.

'He isn't,' I said. 'He loves everybody.'

'You mean God?' she asked.

I didn't, but she'd never understand, so I let it be.

She stopped crying at last and drew me over to the bed, made me sit down and held my hand tightly.

'We'll just have to pick up the pieces,' she said. 'And try to make the best of it. But I've finished with the bastards for good now. This is the bitter end. You'll have to go into one of those Homes, I'll have to find out about them, so no one will be able to point a finger at you, because they'll blame *you* even if the man is a raving lunatic. *He'll* never get blamed, he gets away with murder every time but you're right, it's better to have no husband at all than one who's bonkers. *I* should know. And when the baby is adopted no one need ever know about this, not even Gran. I couldn't stand her poking her nose into this. She'd never understand.'

'I don't want the baby adopted,' I told her.

She looked closely at me. 'Are you feeling all right, Girlie?' she asked. 'Have you been to a doctor yet?'

'No,' I said.

'Well, you'd better see a doctor,' she said. 'It's all this yoga. It's gone to your head. You can't keep a baby who hasn't got a father. Everyone would *know*.'

'I've got on without a father,' I reminded her, 'for much of the time.'

'I was married when I was expecting *you*,' she said. Then she got all serious and worried. 'Is that what it is?' she asked. 'Do you think that that affected you? Do you think you're … well, emotionally scarred?'

I told her no, I thought I was okay, and she jumped up.

'Okay?' she said. 'You're sitting there unmarried and expecting and you think you're okay?' I didn't say anything and she sat down again. 'What do you remember about Dad?' she asked, very seriously. 'I can see now that it must have affected you. It's probably at the bottom of all this. Can you remember how you felt?'

I thought I'd better humour her although I didn't see why

anything had to be at the bottom of anything.

'Well,' I said, 'I remember he just stood there with his mouth all dry, licking his lips with his tongue which was just as dry, so it didn't help at all, and he said to you: "You go your way and I'll go mine." '

'But how do you *feel* about it?' she asked. 'I mean, now?'

'I feel, he's probably happier doing his own thing,' I said. 'I feel okay.'

She got a bit cross again. 'If you feel okay in your situation,' she said, 'you must be in a state of shock. Gran will have something to give you for that but if I ask her she'll want to know what caused the shock, so I'll just make you some Ovaltine and you'd better go to bed. I'll get hold of the university and a doctor and I'll find out about the Home. You just try not to get bitter. Leave everything to me, that's what mothers are for.'

I wasn't getting bitter about anything but I didn't want to argue with her, about the baby or the Home or even the Ovaltine.

I'd drink the Ovaltine, I decided, think about going to a Home, but I knew I wouldn't have to think about keeping the baby.

Mother

I took Girlie to Dr Shaw. I didn't really want to go to him because he knows us, but Girlie insisted that if she was going to a doctor at all, she was going to Dr Shaw because she'd always gone to him and he used to give her a sucker when she was small and I thought it was another sign of shock, her dwelling on the past like that.

So we went and I began to wonder whether Dr Shaw wasn't getting a bit beyond it because he just couldn't see that she was in a state of shock from being ravaged by a maniac like that and having to bear a fatherless child. In fact, he went so far as to say she was in perfect good health.

'But surely,' I said, 'mentally ...'

'And mentally, Iris,' he said. 'Healthy mentally and healthy physically, an out and out healthy, sensible girl, no hysterics, no recriminations, no regrets, a healthy acceptance of the situation, and if things go on as they are now, a healthy baby to show for it.' In a tone of, what more can you ask for? I ask you! But they're all the same. Men always stick together. Especially if they're doctors. Everyone knows that.

'Now I know you're trying to be very brave,' I said to Girlie when we got home. 'But I do think you should have confided in Dr Shaw. After all he was the one who cleared up your nappy rashes and tonsillitis and things like that. He *knows* you. You should have talked to him.'

'But I *did* talk to him,' she said.

'I mean, *talk*. You know what I mean,' I said. I thought I was being very tolerant and understanding, more so than most mothers would have been in the circumstances, but Girlie was beginning to annoy me. I felt she could at least have confided in *me*, she didn't have to pretend to be brave and calm with *me*. 'You didn't tell him how you really feel,' I said. 'About the worry, the anxiety, the fear ... *I* know how you feel,' I told her. 'That's only natural. I'm your mother. But if you'd told him he would have given you some tranquillisers or something to calm you down, something to make you sleep.'

'But I'm *not* worried,' she said. 'And you know I'm sleeping like the dead.'

'Well, that must be nervous tension,' I told her. 'It must be exhausting you. He would have given you something to pep you up if you'd told him.'

Because he *should* have given her something. She was in a state of shock. She had to be, after her awful experience with that long-haired lunatic. It was only natural. I was convinced of it. I'd have to watch her closely until she went into the Home. They'd be expert at dealing with girls who have been outraged and stunned beyond feeling. There'd be someone there to watch her all the time, and the more I thought about it the more convinced I was that the sooner she went, the better. They'd know the difference there between someone who was healthy and someone who was stunned beyond feeling, sleeping and acting brave all the time, when they might even be close to suicide.

So much for Dr Shaw. And I'd have to tell Gran she was going into residence at the university, or better still, going to another university, where she'd *have* to go into residence.

And thinking about everything I had to do, in the state of shock that *I* was in, I began to be sorry that I hadn't got something from Dr Shaw for myself.

2

Gran

'It's nothing short of disgusting,' I told Iris, 'the youth of today. Esmé McKechnie was saying on the stairs only this morning that they're not satisfied with being teenagers any more, they've got to be hippies and beatniks so they never wash and the airlines don't want to take them on board the way they smell. She was mentioning about mobs of them camping out in parks overseas, messing the place up, but I told her that's one thing we've got to thank the government for because Esmé is always down on the government. We've got to thank them for keeping us backward and clean-living, I told her, which was a mistake because she said oh, is that so and by the way, how's that boy with the long hair and old tyres on his feet who came visiting Girlie? I told her there was nothing in *that*, he only came once or twice and he was going fishing that day he was wearing old tyres and he was going to drop in at the barber's on the way home, but I was that ashamed, so I enquired how her young Patrick was getting on, still blocking the toilets and wetting floors? Because we've all got skeletons, haven't we?'

But Iris just went on sitting there saying nothing with that glazed look she'd got lately so I changed the subject to try and take her out of herself.

'And what's all this I hear about Women's Lib?' I asked her, thinking: that'll give her something to think about. 'What are all these women going on about?'

She rouses herself then like that was all she was waiting for and says: 'Women are not free, like men.'

'Free?' I asked her. 'Whoever's free in this vale of sorrow?'

'Men can do what they damn well like,' she says, 'but women have to bear the consequences.'

I was glad she was roused out of herself, but I've never

known Iris so fierce, and she's my own daughter; I thought, her thinking's wrong somewhere, and it was up to me to put it right, so I told her: 'Men have homes and wives and families, they can't do as they like, they've got to work to keep them.'

'Well, it's the women who have got to have the babies,' she says, with a crack in her voice, like she's had half a dozen herself instead of one and someone was asking her to have half a dozen more.

'That's only nature,' I said. 'What can they do about that? They can't change that.'

'No, but that's what's so *unfair*,' she says, and her bottom lip and her chin start quivering.

'Here, what's up with you?' I asked her.

'Nothing,' she says. 'It's just that men can do what they like, but it's the girl who has to have the babies.'

'Well, what's she getting married for then if she doesn't want babies?' I asked her, because Iris was making even less sense than usual.

'I mean if she *isn't* married,' Iris wails.

Well, I never knew that Iris felt so strongly about that sort of thing which is a scandal and a disgrace and a tragedy, of course, but what did it have to do with *us*?

'That's Women's Lib,' I said. 'They want gels to sleep around when they're not married, but that's fornication, as the Bible says, and it's a sin!'

'That doesn't *help*!' Iris yells and she leaps up.

Well, she's my own daughter, but I swear I'll never understand Iris. 'Here,' I said. 'What are you going on about? There's not much Women's Lib here, and that's another thing we've got to thank the government for, which I may mention to Esmé tomorrow.' But Iris just stands there biting her lip.

'Iris,' I said. 'You're not worrying about all *that*, are you? You're not worrying about Women's Lib and Girlie?' But that was too ridiculous, even for Iris. 'For heaven's sake,' I said. 'Get a hold on yourself. Girlie knows all the facts of life. Just you put fear of the devil into her, about getting VD and having a baby and all that, like I did with you, and you'll not have any cause to worry.'

I thought Iris was going to say something, but she just rushed out. She's always rushing out these days, no matter what I say. I'm beginning to think she's starting the change of life early. Some women do get taken up in funny ways. Then again, I thought, no. But there was something going on with Iris and Girlie. Something fishy that I didn't know about. Because it was bound to be fishy if they weren't letting me in on it.

Mother

I just couldn't get over it. For the first fifteen months of her life I read nothing but Spock. It actually fell to pieces in the end. So where had I gone wrong? But it takes two to tango. *His* mother probably didn't read Spock. Not that it would help, knowing that now, but I couldn't help thinking along those lines when I went to the Home for Unmarried Mothers, because *I* was the one who was having to go there and not *his* mother.

The place looked sort of shut up from the outside, like a jail, and the Secretary had a closed look about him too. He made a big thing of the love and understanding the girls received there, as if none of them could possibly have had that before and he looked surprised when I told him Girlie had been living at home all the time, because, he said, most of the girls they had there had come from farms and country areas to the city where they were not supervised, and he gave a tight little smile when I said well, Girlie *was* supervised, and he cocked his head with a come, come, look because of course if she *had* been supervised I wouldn't have been there would I?

I said: 'You can't watch them *all* the time,' and he said no, but it was the basic upbringing that counted, wasn't it?

Still, he admitted, girls do go off the rails, and did I realise

108

that bearing children out of wedlock was a heartbreaking experience and the worst part was having to give up the baby? Because she *was* giving up the baby? I said yes, I thought so, and he said:

'You *think* so and she's only eighteen, still a student and not married?' With a tight little smile, implying, I suppose, that with such a breakdown in communication between Girlie and me, anything could happen and obviously already had.

I didn't want to argue with him or antagonise him if I was going to get Girlie into the place so I said nothing and he went on: had she been given a firm religious background? I said yes, thinking Gran had done her best, which was considerable, and wondering whether all the yoga and meditation since then could be counted too, and he looked very surprised again, because, he said, it was girls who did not have a firm religious background who fell into evil ways.

I couldn't let that pass. 'She hasn't exactly fallen into evil ways,' I said. 'She must have thought she was in love with this boy and ...'

His tight little smile cut me off. If I didn't consider that evil ways, if my own morals were *that* lax, he hinted with a hopeless little shrug ... well then ...

I had been feeling awfully guilty and misunderstood and I began to feel a little angry as well. After all, *I* was a married mother, or at least a divorced mother, and I'd done my best for Girlie, but before I could say anything more he stood up and asked if I'd like to talk to the Matron.

I didn't like him and I didn't like his place, but I thought I'd better see the Matron before I made up my mind because the Matron would, after all, have more to do with the girls than the Secretary.

I was glad I did, because I liked her at once, probably because her smile was open and real and she looked motherly, a little bit like Gran when she was in a good mood, in fact.

'The girls are very happy here,' she told me. 'We encourage them to spend their waiting time in handwork and knitting.

From time to time we sell the articles at fêtes to raise funds. Everyone works together and for leisure there are weekly outings, the radio and we're hoping to get a projector. There's a tuck shop too, so a little spending-money ...?'

That would be all right, I said, quite all right. Spending-money was the least of it.

Still smiling, the Matron led me into her office and offered me tea.

'Now,' she said, 'would you like to tell me all about it?'

I didn't really know all about it. I'd only seen that boy a couple of times and now Girlie was expecting, so I said: 'Well, my daughter's expecting.'

The Matron smiled. 'I understand,' she said, 'but you must tell me all about it because the girls are usually too upset to talk and it helps if we know a little bit about the background.'

'Well, there was this boy,' I said. 'He's since left town. I don't think and he was quite all there. But then, they do all sorts of queer things these days. Anyway, they must have gone too far.'

'Obviously,' the Matron said, and she smiled even harder. 'But you had better tell me *everything*.'

Well, I said, trying hard to be cooperative, I don't think this boy knew Girlie was expecting when he left.'

'That is immaterial,' the Matron said. 'It's the *why* that's important, not the *who*. For instance, in our experience, which is naturally considerable, an unhappy home is a bigger cause of girls getting into trouble than malnutrition, poverty, low intelligence or living apart from their parents. Now what ...'

'Oh, none of those,' I said, and I had to ask her: 'Don't they ever just fall in love with the boys?'

'In love?' The Matron's smile was beginning to show signs of strain. 'I suppose so, but then they would have to be very misguided, wouldn't they?' I thought about him, that long-haired boy with his sandals and sitar and I had to agree.

'Now,' the Matron said, 'How is her father reacting to this?'

'He isn't here either,' I told her. 'I'm divorced.' I was surprised at how grim she looked without that smile, grimmer than Gran could ever look, even in the worst of her moods.

'Well, at least,' she said, as though trying to make the best of a really bad situation, 'at least you haven't rejected her or you wouldn't be here. That might help a bit. Our first responsibility must be towards the girls. You should realise that they feel intensely alone. The fact that they are not supported by husbands strikes at their very hearts. Naturally they feel terribly guilty and ashamed and rejected. They feel lost and desperate, and the giving away of the baby, well, that is the price they have to pay. We do all we can for them but naturally they still suffer a great deal. Religious instruction helps, of course.'

The Matron had stopped looking at me ever since she'd heard I was divorced. She looked at the ceiling while she spoke and I felt I'd have to talk quite loudly if I was going to gain her attention, but I simply had to know:

'If they're not worried or guilty or anything like that, do you think they could be in a state of shock?'

Her smile came back as though she'd been expecting to hear just that. 'Your daughter doesn't feel bad then?' she asked.

'No,' I told her apologetically, 'she seems to be feeling rather good.'

'And you say her intelligence is normal?'

'Oh yes,' I said. 'She's doing rather well at the university.'

'And she's had firm religious instruction?'

'Quite firm,' I said, thinking Gran's instruction had been very firm even if her theology was a bit shaky. 'I think she must be in a state of shock.'

'Well, we'll soon pull her out of *that*,' the Matron said.

'Oh, but do you think you should?' I asked, because I wasn't so sure, if it was going to mean that Girlie would spend her waiting time feeling intensely alone and guilty and suffering a great deal.

'Unless,' the Matron said grimly, 'you want this to happen

to her again?' and I shook my head, because I didn't.

'Well then, what we do,' she said, 'is to instil a proper set of values into them so that they take their places in society and never ever fall again.'

I left after that and I thought, that was all right as far as it went, but I decided to have a look at the other places too because I kept seeing Girlie's face, vague and dreamy, without a hint of guilt or shadow of worry, six or seven months pregnant and deserted but without any rancour or resentment. I knew she had to be in a state of shock; either that or that beatnik with the bell had brainwashed her.

But I didn't want her pulled out of it by that Matron and loaded up with loneliness and desperation. And she *was* sorry, I could see she was. For one thing she kept bringing me cups of tea, weak and slopped all over the saucer as usual, but it was the thought that counted.

Girlie

I didn't want to go into any Home, but Mother was so uptight about everything that I had to. So while she was going around looking at them I sat in the park so Gran would think I was at lectures, until Mother found a place for me.

It was all squared off and landscaped in the park, horribly controlled and confined but still a lot better than the concrete and tarmac that Vern said were like scabs on the earth. Although out in the open even the tarmac was different, he said. It was almost alive, it looped along like a switchback or stretched far ahead, shimmering with mirages, making you feel you'd come from nowhere and would go on for ever, never getting anywhere.

I watched the people in the park and I wished that Vern was there to talk to me, to tell me about the things he'd seen and things he'd thought because he told them like no one else could, and saw things that no one else did.

Other people were always on about the Africans ruining the land and wanting more when they couldn't develop what they had and the state the shops were in now that the white advisers didn't go round any more, about how they stopped working and the shops were closing down. But Vern said standing behind a counter in a stuffy shop wasn't his bag either. As for the roads, it was true they just dumped stone and rubble down in the middle and hoped the cars would flatten it all out, only they went round so it was like an obstacle course, Vern said, real-life Dodgems.

He liked rapping with Africans. They were like ancient Britons, he said, happy to paddle their coracles with their bottoms painted blue, leaving to the Romans all the sweat with the aqueducts and things.

He said he wasn't texture- or goal-orientated, but of the two he much preferred the former, which was why he felt the vibes were good amongst the ordinary Africans but bad in the white cities, some worse than others, like Pretoria, where they'd got bronze buck standing on their soft noses holding up urns with their horns and a bust balancing on its Adam's apple with concrete billowing over it like a spinnaker. He always split before he could get used to it, he said, before it stopped bugging him.

Vern could make everything interesting; he could have made even the dreary park come alive. He wouldn't even have to say anything. It just wouldn't have been so dreary, if he had been there.

Mother

The second Home I saw looked much better. It had a lovely big garden, and because it was enclosed by a very high hedge, some of the pregnant girls were walking about outside. I thought it looked very nice. It didn't look so closed up.

The Matron was an elderly spinster, very serious and dedicated. She didn't smile at all and she told me at once that eighty per cent of her girls came from broken homes. I nodded meekly. What else could I do?

'However,' she said, 'we are not here to reproach or condemn.' I appreciated that, so I nodded again.

'Only to help,' she told me severely. 'Many people,' she said, 'have erroneous ideas about our organisation,' and she looked at me closely to see if I was one of them.

'But we understand the problems of the girls and most of all we *keep their secret.*'

I said that that was just what I was trying to do.

'The babies are put up for adoption,' she said, 'and are assured of a happy future.'

I nodded my enthusiastic approval, but the Matron ignored me.

'Every case is treated confidentially,' she said, 'so there is no need for desperate action at all.'

That brought me up a bit. 'Desperate action?' I asked, wondering who she had in mind, Girlie or me.

'Young unmarried girls,' the Matron said solemnly, 'suffer tremendous emotional upheaval before and after the birth. They become terribly depressed. They feel that life is not worth living. They should never be left on their own because you will understand that their terrible depression can lead to precipitous action. Who is watching her now?'

'Now?' I stammered. 'She's in the park just now, but really, I don't think ... I mean, Girlie's not like that, I would have noticed, I'm sure ...'

The Matron nodded knowingly. 'We must remember that an experience like this unhinges girls. They may not be looking as unhinged as they are feeling. We, of course, are expert at helping them to bring their true feelings to the surface, to express their terrible fears and depressions.'

'Oh, but *unhinged,*' I protested, 'I don't think that Girlie ...'

I realised at once that the Matron didn't like to be contradicted. She half closed her eyes and ignored me. 'I often think,' she said, 'that if the divorce courts ran films of some of our unmarried mothers-to-be, depressed, unhinged ... those who are lucky enough to *get* here, which is not taking into account the tragic cases who *don't* get here, who *are* in fact driven to desperate action ...'

I thanked her and left as soon as I could. I was feeling pretty unhinged myself by then. Two things had been brought home to me: as the divorced mother of an unmarried mother-to-be I was morally more culpable than she was, and Girlie, unless I was terribly mistaken, was not a typical unmarried expectant mother at all. She was too guiltless. She wasn't desperate enough. She had to be in a state of shock, unless ... and then another possibility struck me: if she weren't in a state of shock then she probably knew that boy was going to come back. That would explain why she wasn't depressed and suffering and desperate, why she thought she could keep the baby. And if that were true it would mean a very quiet marriage, maybe even a marriage after the event, but it would solve the whole problem. After all, he couldn't be all *that* bad, not if Girlie thought she loved him. A bit eccentric perhaps, but there were lots of eccentric men who settled down to make very good husbands.

My own desperate depression started to lift a little. I couldn't wait to get home to ask Girlie, to insist once and for all on the truth about that boy, but when I did she seemed surprised.

'But I *told* you,' she said. 'I don't know.'

'Well, if you don't *know*, then he *may* come back?'

'I don't *know*,' she said. 'Why, anyway?'

'Why,' I said, gritting my teeth to keep my voice down and feeling my nostrils flaring, 'is that I'm having to go around getting myself humiliated and insulted by self-righteous know-it-all Matrons at Homes for Unmarried Mothers when all *I* ever did was get divorced.'

'Hell, Mother,' Girlie said, and I must admit that she sounded genuinely sympathetic. 'I don't want you to go around getting yourself insulted. Fag the Homes. I don't want to go anyway.'

'Oh you don't!' I started, but then I heard Gran coming down the passage so I grabbed a pillow and threw it at her instead, as hard as I could. She didn't say anything. Maybe she'd heard Gran coming too, or maybe she understood how I was feeling because she picked the pillow up and put it back on the bed and said she was going to make me a nice cup of tea.

3

Gran

Iris was charging around like an old warhorse with a burr in its backside and Girlie spent most of her time sitting with her toes curled around her legs giving herself bunions before her time and neither one of them had a thought for poor old Emily, but I kept her in mind, wondering how the operation went off and when she'd be back. I remembered her in my prayers too and thought it's a pity the people overseas don't know about that. Low wages is all they can think about but the cost of living is higher there and everyone knows that the natives' standard of living is low and they'd just spend the extra money on clothes or transistor radios or those big flashy watches they don't need because time means nothing to them anyway.

So there I was waiting and worrying until at last the letter came that I had asked the doctor in East London to write to me and I had to read it three times before I could believe it:

> *Your maid Emily Mazwi came to my office this morning and handed me your envelope. She was examined at Outpatients, advised an operation and offered immediate admission. This she declined and has gone off to think it over. One can understand her feelings but there will be some delay now – and the next move is up to her.*

It was signed by a Dr Somebody-or-other, I couldn't make it out, and 'Frere Hospital'.

Well, I just couldn't believe it so I went over to Esmé McKechnie at once and gave it to her to read.

'Can you get over it?' I asked her. 'She *went* there to have the operation that's what she *went* for, and now she has to think it over, but she'd thought it over *here* and that's why she went *there*.'

Esmé read the letter and then she said: 'Doctor who?'

'That isn't the *point*,' I said. Esmé always was a nit-picker. 'She couldn't walk for the pain and they offered her a bed *straightaway*!'

Esmé gave the letter back to me. 'That's these people all over,' she said. 'You never know how their minds work.'

'And we gave her all those nighties and that bedjacket with all that fine knitting in it for the *operation*.'

'If you're going to let these people upset you,' Esmé said, 'you're never going to see the end of it.'

'Offered an expensive operation like that for nothing,' I said, 'and it isn't good enough for her. If it had been any of us we'd have had to pay. It's almost enough to make one vote for the government. It just goes to show: oil and water don't mix.' Oh, I was really seething, after the way I'd been praying for her.

'Well, what now?' Esmé asked.

'That's what I'd like to know,' I said. 'Is she going to come back without the operation, after all those prayers? I wonder what the Good Lord thinks about *that*?'

We showed the letter to Mrs Merriman and Mrs Goedhals and I expected Mrs Goedhals to go off pop because she votes for the government, but she didn't funnily enough, she just nodded. I couldn't make out if she had been expecting it or was agreeing with it or what, so I asked her:

'Well, what do you think about it?' and she said:

'To think is one thing but a still tongue is better.'

There was nothing we could say to that. I've always thought Mrs Goedhals is deeper than she looks, but Esmé says it's all put-on and show-off. In any case, there was nothing we could do but wait, at least until the three weeks we had given Emily were up, and then find someone else.

But in the meantime I was getting lumbago from having to go down on my hands and knees all the time. Iris told me for heaven's sake to leave the floors, she would do them over the weekend, because Girlie wasn't to bend down too much, she'd ricked her back or something, and I said I was surprised her toes weren't ricked as well, the way she was always curling them up. But I couldn't leave the floors until the weekend. As soon as you start leaving floors you get cockroaches and once you get them you're overrun before you know where you are.

Mother

When I saw the third Home I knew it was the one. It was also privately run –the provincial place had a long waiting list, I'd been told – and it was quite expensive, but as ideal, I thought, as a place like that could ever be.

The elegant Matron didn't even hint at guilt, depression or suicide. Here, I was told, Girlie would be taught her responsibilities, become mature and adjust mentally and emotionally to her changed circumstances. It sounded very promising and I asked to be shown around. There was a library, recreation and sewing rooms where the girls played games and were taught handcrafts and needlework. They also learnt simple cooking and shorthand and typing. The bedrooms, single and double, were airy and pleasant. In the largest recreation room they were given deportment and charm lessons and did their prenatal exercises. They were encouraged to pursue hobbies like painting and playing the guitar and piano and there was even a swimming pool. In the evenings, the Matron told me, there were beetle drives, discussions, films and debates. Special arrangements were made for those girls who wished to continue with their schooling and a psychologist came once a week to iron out any personal problems.

It sounded like a posh Finishing School, until the matter of the babies came up.

'No girl is ever forced to give up her baby for adoption,' the Matron told me. 'Where arrangements can be made with crèches to care for the baby while the mother is working, if their families cannot or will not help them, the girls are encouraged and supported in their decision. For the majority of course,' she added sadly, 'this is not possible, but then adoption is arranged with the least possible trauma to the unfortunate mother.'

The girls, she went on, were all very happy and I said I could see that. 'In fact,' she said, 'they often return to express their appreciation or just to visit the staff who are all highly qualified, most of them specialists in their fields.'

I rushed home to tell Girlie but she was helping Gran with supper so I had to wait until Gran went to bed, which began to seem like never.

When I finally had the chance to talk to Girlie alone I told her all about it, the deportment classes and the charm classes and the swimming pool and the beetle drives. I said it was just like a holiday resort and she could go on with her studies there too, and she said, some holiday resort with studies.

'Now, the Matron is charming,' I told her, 'and it's an expensive place but you'll get good care and exercises.'

I made it sound very nice, I thought, but Girlie just sat there. She didn't even nod.

'You won't feel bad at all,' I said, 'because everyone there is in the same boat.'

'I don't feel bad now,' she said, 'and if I stayed at home it wouldn't cost anything.'

I started gritting my teeth again and I longed, I really ached, to be able to raise my voice and get some of it out of my system.

'If you don't feel bad,' I gritted at her, 'it's because you don't consider anybody but yourself. And you're going. It's all arranged. You've got to think of Gran's feelings, and the neighbours' feelings and my feelings and my job and the gossiping and whispering and the scandal.'

'And what about the baby?' she asked me. 'Everyone's going to know anyway.'

'No,' I said. 'They'll help you to sort that out at the Home. You've got to give it up of course, you're not married, that's settled, and they've got specialists there to make it easy, you won't feel a thing, the Matron said so.'

Girlie began to go red in the face, and I thought, one hurdle at a time, so I said: 'The Matron did say they don't actually force anybody to do anything.'

'Cross your heart?' Girlie asked.

'Cross my heart,' I said.

'And if I don't like it, I can come home?'

I hesitated, but then I decided, of course she'll like it. It's just like a Finishing School, all those beetle drives and things, she was going to love it, charm classes and everything and that elegant, understanding Matron, so I said yes, and she said again:

'Cross your heart?'

And I said: 'Cross my heart.'

'And what about Gran?' she asked.

I had already thought about that. 'We'll tell her you're going to another university, into residence. That's almost the truth anyway. You'll see, this place is just like a small private college.' And it was, only I couldn't help feeling guilty, even though I had nothing to feel guilty about. It must have been the look on Girlie's face and the way she had pleaded with me to cross my heart, like she used to do when she was small. She made me feel as if somehow I was betraying her.

'Listen,' I said, 'you are going to *try* to like it there?'

She hesitated and then she said: 'Yes.'

'Cross your heart?'

'Cross my heart,' she said, because that was an understanding we'd always had and it was binding between us.

Girlie

I didn't want to go. I was sweating scared at the thought of a place like that. I didn't have much courage. I wasn't like Vern. I asked him once, wasn't he scared, going off like that and maybe running out of bread, but he said no, it wasn't courage, it was a lack of self-concern, it was self-denial, *tapas*, so there couldn't be any fear. Self-concern, he said, led to fear and all the other evils, like pride and murder and war. Denial of self and love for others, he said, was the single truth all the great religions had in common.

Vern was up on all the great religions. I found it difficult because Gran had drummed it into me that our church was the only one. I remember Vern smiling at me like he knew what I was thinking because he started telling me about this guru who denied he even *had* a theology and disbanded his followers because he believed that one leader could give only one aspect of the whole truth. I was trying to get all that when Vern said:

'But words are useless when it comes to discussing the absolute truth,' which seemed to me to lead just nowhere. Then he said: 'A girl is walking down the street, is she the younger or the older sister?'

'What's that supposed to mean?' I asked him.

'That's a koan,' Vern said, 'it shows how inadequate words really are and how they can be meaningless.'

'But there's got to be a meaning,' I said.

'There *is* a meaning,' he said. 'Meditate, recite your mantra and you will gradually lose self-concern and eventually find the meaning. That's when you get there, when you achieve *samadhi*, complete unity of the soul with the reality, but *tapas*, lack of self-concern, must come first.'

So I tried that, to practise *tapas*, to lose my fear of going to that Home, or even just to reach the stage where I could *think* of going which I did, finally, but only after reciting an awful lot of mantras, my own, every single other one I knew, and even a few I made up myself.

4

Gran

I had to talk to Iris so I waited until Girlie had gone to bed, which she is doing very early these days and I don't know if that's altogether right, as I told her, you're only young once and you don't want to sleep the best years of your life away, but all that was beside the point. The point was that I waited because I do think a little bit of tact goes a long way, so as soon as Girlie was in bed I said to Iris:

'Maybe a still tongue does make a wise head but there are limits to everything, like the way she's moping around these days, you're sure she hasn't got a fever or something?'

'What?' Iris says. I was beginning to think she must have a fever or something as well. Maybe they both had something or other, in which case I would probably catch it too, and come to think of it, I was feeling a bit washed out myself lately, but I had put it down to the weather.

'I said, a still tongue makes a wise head,' I started again.

'For God's sake, what do you keep talking about tongues and heads for?' Iris asks, all in a pet, without giving me a chance to finish, but I kept my patience.

'A still tongue does make a wise head,' I said, 'but it's getting a bit much the way Girlie is slopping and moping around not saying anything. It isn't as though she's got worries at her age, and I suggest you think twice before you take the Lord's name in vain, Iris.'

She put her book down. I knew she wasn't reading it because she hadn't turned the page once since she'd sat down.

'Actually, I wanted to talk to you about Girlie,' she says to me.

'And about time too,' I said. 'I don't know what's wrong with that gel, but she's got that silly look on her face and she sits there humming om, om, om to herself as if she's hearing music from somewhere. It's not right. And her neck. Have you seen her neck lately?'

'Her neck?' and she gives a high sort of laugh. 'I haven't been looking at her *neck*,' she says, as though there was something else to look at.

'Well, cleanliness is next to Godliness, I told her. And I said, it won't hurt you to wash your neck occasionally. It's got a tidemark like a dirty bath around it.'

Iris gives that sharp nervous laugh again. 'Oh,' she says, 'that's always been like that. What I wanted to tell you is that I'm sending her away, to another university, so she'll live in the residence.'

Right out of the blue she says it and not a word about it before and no connection that I could see with Girlie's neck.

'You tell me right out of the blue like that?' I asked her, and I thought, Iris must have something worse than a fever.

'Well,' she says, 'she'll like it. It'll get her away from us for a bit, she'll stand on her own two feet and ...'

'You must be out of your mind,' I told her, 'stand on her own two feet when she can't even keep her neck clean. Who's going to remind her about her neck in a residence? It's like sending someone to a boarding school and as far as I know it's only problem children that get sent there.'

'Well,' Iris says, suddenly all terribly nice and reasonable, which always makes me suspicious. 'She'll have to learn all that, to do for herself, it'll do her good, living among young people of her own age and all that.'

'And what about the money?' I asked her, because I smelt a rat somewhere only I didn't know where. 'Residence isn't cheap. You can hardly afford the tuition here with her living at home. And where is this university?'

'Oh,' Iris says, and I can see she's thinking hard which makes me even more suspicious. 'Away from here altogether, Grahamstown, maybe Cape Town ...'

'And how are you going to visit her?' I asked.

'Well, it's just for a little while,' Iris says, 'to see if she likes it, an experiment. We needn't go and visit her.'

'And the holidays?' I asked, to see if Iris was really serious, to see if she'd thought this thing through properly.

'She may not want to come home right away,' Iris says, 'at least, not for the first holidays, you never know, she'll make friends, she may want to spend the holidays with a little friend, you never know.'

There was something fishy about it somewhere but I just couldn't put been my finger on it. 'You'll let her go to university in Cape Town which costs a fortune and not go and see her over the weekends and let her spend the holidays heaven knows where with a friend you don't even know?' And then I knew what it was, the rat that I'd been smelling. 'Iris,' I said, 'you're getting married again. Is that it?'

She looked at me, surprised, and then she laughed so hard, a funny, hurtful sort of laugh, that the book fell right off her lap.

'You're getting married,' I said. 'So you'll have money and you're getting rid of Girlie. And it'll be me next. Oh, Iris, I ...'

'No,' she said. 'No, I'm not, and I don't know what I'm laughing about. God knows I've got nothing to laugh about.'

'I should say not,' I said. But I never really seriously believed she was getting married again because I would have known. Iris could never have kept anything like that secret from me. 'Well, what's it all about then?' I asked her, determined to make her stop her nonsense. 'Just come straight out with it. It started with Girlie's neck, now what ...'

'It didn't,' Iris says. 'Her neck's got nothing to do with it, God knows.'

I got a bit annoyed then. 'Stop talking in riddles and taking the Lord's name in vain,' I said. 'You've been talking in riddles and going around in circles and laughing your head off about nothing all night long, now what's the matter with you?'

'There's nothing the matter with *me*,' she says, 'I only wish there was. And if all I'm doing is talking riddles it's a miracle because it's a wonder I haven't gone off my head.'

'That's just it,' I said. 'Maybe you *are* off your head. For instance, what's all this nonsense about Girlie going away to university? She's at a perfectly good university right here.'

'All that's settled,' Iris says. 'It's been fixed. She's going, she's got a friend, her best friend went there and she'll spend the holidays with her, so it's all settled.'

Just like that, all settled, and not a word about it to me until now.

'Well, I don't know about those residences,' I warned her. 'I don't like to say it because Girlie's an ordinary healthy girl even if she can't keep her neck clean, but I've heard about those places.'

Iris's head snaps up. 'What places?' she asks, and I thought again, there's something fishy about the whole business.

'Residences,' I said. 'Aren't we talking about residences?'

'Yes of course,' she says, 'residences,' and I began to wonder whether a bit of Wincarnis now and then wouldn't be better for her instead of that gin which must be affecting her liver although heaven knew she was acting more as if it was affecting her head.

'I don't like to say it,' I said, 'but sometimes it can be unhealthy, if a gel like Girlie who's always lived at home suddenly gets cut loose. You'll want to think about that, Iris,' I told her. 'There'll be boys ...'

'She's had quite enough of boys already,' Iris snaps, and I didn't know what *that* was supposed to mean, but I decided to get Girlie's side of the story because there was a rat somewhere that I kept smelling, and I'm good at that, smelling rats, so I went in to speak to Girlie while Iris was in the bathroom getting ready for bed.

She was wool-gathering as usual, but at least she was on her back instead of her haunches.

'I hear you're suddenly going away,' I said. 'Your mother has very kindly told me at last. Of course I knew something was going on with you and her whispering all over the place, but I do like to be told these things. Now, do you really want to go? You can tell your Gran. Your Gran's always been on your side, you know that.'

Girlie shrugged, or rather, wriggled, since she was lying down. 'Oh that,' she said. 'Yes.'

'Because of this friend of yours?' I asked. 'You're sure? Which friend? Who is she?'

'My friend,' Girlie said. 'Oh, my friend, that's … Verna.'

'Never heard of her,' I said. 'Who's Verna? You're quite sure you want to go? It'll be costing your mother quite a bit, you know. She'll likely be dipping into her little bit of savings.'

'I know,' Girlie said. 'But I'd better go.'

I went to bed myself then. I didn't want to talk to Iris any more, not after the way she had kept this business from me. It wasn't like her, and I wondered what we were coming to, why we couldn't trust each other any more to thrash things out between us like we used to.

Mother

After Girlie had gone I just let myself go. I went to work automatically and I came home automatically, I bickered with Gran automatically and I went to bed automatically. But I couldn't sleep. I kept telling myself it was all right, Girlie was in the Home, and when the baby was adopted no one would know. Not even Gran, and if *she* didn't know then no one would know.

It didn't help much. Maybe I felt so empty inside because I was missing Girlie so much and because I had nothing of my own, no life of my own, no letters even any more, not that they had been worth much.

It's because I never get out, I thought. But there wasn't anywhere to go. You couldn't go anywhere on your own, not even to see a film, without feeling odd, except in the afternoon and then the place was full of kids and other women on their own trying to pretend they're independent and coming to terms all right.

I could hardly remember when last I'd been to a party because women aren't invited to parties on their own like men. An extra man livens things up but an extra woman just creates tension if she's pretty, and pity if she isn't. Unless they're deliberately trying to pair you off with someone and then there's usually something wrong with him, there always is if other people have got to scratch around to pair him off, like that whatever-his-name-was that I simply had to meet, Lillian at the office said. She was going to lay the whole thing on. He wasn't handsome, but he was a real honey, she said. He certainly wasn't handsome; in fact he had big buck teeth with gaps between them and I wouldn't even have minded that so much except that he kept scraping them across my cheek like a garden rake when he thought no one was looking, and halfway through the evening I had streaks of make-up missing so that my face looked like a Venetian blind.

And if that sort of thing didn't happen there was always trouble with men and their wives, like that time Midge – they called him that, I remember, because he was so tall – danced with me all the time, pinching my nipples. I didn't even know he was married until he stopped dead and said: 'My old woman! She must have gone off home again!' and he rushed off, leaving me flat on the floor with pins and needles in my nipples.

And the divorced men, and the widowed, didn't want to get caught again. They'd make you feel warm and nice and ask if they could take you home but halfway there it was always what about coming to my place for a drink? And maybe it's for the night, maybe it's an affair, but they didn't want anything serious, and I just couldn't do it with anybody and everybody. Maybe that was why I had this question in my mind about Girlie all the time: how many of them? But I couldn't ask her because I didn't want to know. Maybe sex was getting more casual but I wasn't. And I'd never change. I was too old for that now.

There are those youth pills that are supposed to revitalise you, make you lose weight and make your breathing easier, but there's nothing wrong with my breathing. Not yet anyway. I thought, maybe Phoebe should take them if she isn't too far gone already. In any case I wanted someone to revitalise myself for; I didn't want to revitalise myself for myself. If it was just for myself I might as well get old and be done with it.

Not that one had any choice, and that made me feel even more morbid, and not being able to sleep, I made a list of the signs of old age creeping on so that I could feel even more morbid: sore feet if you don't wear sensible shoes at least half a size bigger than you used to, only looking nice in tailored clothes that cost the earth, policemen looking younger than you do, which is a music-hall joke but true enough, your eyes ruined for days after half an hour's crying, and one of the worst signs, I suppose, was lying awake at night making lists like that.

I'd got myself so morbid by then that I had to try and think about something else. But all I could think of was something I'd read somewhere: people are only as old as their arteries. Not that that helped much.

Next morning I said to Gran: 'I feel terrible. I must be getting old.'

'That's arrant nonsense,' she said. 'I'm nearly twice as old as you are and I don't feel old because I accept my problems. That's what life is all about.'

And maybe she was right. Maybe it was the way I was trying to fight my problems that was making me feel old. But I'd been doing it for so long that I couldn't stop. I didn't know how to.

5

Gran

I was having a cup of coffee with Mrs Goedhals because you can say what you like about the Afrikaans people but they do brew a good cup of coffee, none of this instant stuff for them, only she was cleaning some tripe and trotters and that almost put me off, the muck she was scraping off the tripe and the way she was scratching to get the hair out from between the toes and talking all the time about the old Boer recipes like bredies and sugar-beans and yellow rice and stiff mealie-meal porridge and boerewors and samp and sour milk which I thought was natives' food. Perhaps that's why they understand each other so well.

But at least Mrs Goedhals wasn't doing a head. Heads were scarce in the city, she said, which I couldn't understand, because where there's tripe and trotters there must be a head somewhere, but I was glad because I really can't stand that, all that scraping and poking in the nostrils and ears and the look of those dead yellow teeth. I don't know how the Goedhalses can eat it. I prefer some nice clean tinned salmon myself. At least that doesn't look at you with dead eyes.

I had another cup of coffee and I was still with her when Esmé McKechnie came in with a letter for me which she must have nearly dislocated her fingers fishing out of our letter box.

'East London,' she said. 'It must be from Emily.'

We were all glad to hear from her at last, just to get that business settled, so I read it out:

Dear Old Madam and all the other Madams, I think you have been waiting to hear from EL. I mean from me. Now the Doctor said there are things growing and there is a big one and small ones so it will not be good to cut it off because the small ones will grow but they are not so bad and the only thing they will shorten my life. And as my sister wasn't here she was at King. We decided to leave it seeing it's not worrying me and it may take another time to get the bed. And how are you all there. I don't know if I must come back October or the 26th. I think I may stay and we can talk it over when I am back. Course I want to have a good rest. With best regards to all, Bye Bye, Emily.

We all just looked at each other for a while and then Esmé said: 'So she wants to have a good rest. And what about us?'

'And she's not even had the operation,' I said.

'Big things and small things growing inside her that are going to shorten her life and she says she's all right!' Esmé said.

'And we gave her nighties and bedjackets,' I said.

Mrs Goedhals nodded as though she had been expecting it all along and poured us another cup of coffee. 'It reminds me of that old story about the turkeys and the mageu,' she said. 'Or maybe it was mamele. You must have heard it.'

We said no and waited for her to tell it because Mrs Goedhals knew what she was talking about. She grew up on a farm with these people and we knew that if anyone could understand Emily's behaviour it would be Mrs Goedhals.

'It was just before Christmas,' she said, 'and the natives were making mageu, or mamele, from corn, very strong but it was clean in those days, not like the skokiaan they put battery acid in today, a whole few paraffin tins full. It wasn't allowed so when it was found out they had to empty it all out and you know, they emptied it over the turkeys' food. It must have been spite because it's a lot of trouble making that mageu or mamele, and a few hours later there were the turkeys, lying on their backs with their feet up in the air. So the story goes, the old boy, Tone – he had six toes on his feet you know and that's unlucky and they wanted to kill him when he was a baby because they thought the mamtolsi put a spell on him – he had to pluck the turkeys and put them in the kitchen and then chase all the other natives off the farm. And then right in the middle of the night, there was this scratching, scratching and there were all the turkeys with no feathers on, falling around, still drunk from the mageu or mamele. So you see there comes the time when you've got to sack them all.'

I didn't really see what drunk turkeys had to do with Emily's operation, except that we would have to sack her too. But Mrs Goedhals knows what she's talking about, she grew up with these people.

She offered us some more coffee but the tripe was beginning to boil smelling like dirty dishcloths, so I said no, I had better go and write to Emily and warn her not to come back without the operation, after we had given her all those nighties and things.

Mother

When I got home Gran was looking so self-satisfied that I knew at once that something was wrong so I poured a gin and waited for her to come out with it which she always does in her own good time and eventually she said:

'Well, she's back.'

'Who?' I asked. 'Emily?'

'Emily?' Gran snorted. 'Your daughter, that's who. She's back.'

I slopped a lot of gin and had to sit down. 'Girlie?' I asked stupidly.

'Girlie.' And I could see that Gran was enjoying herself. 'Chance of going into residence at a good university to strengthen her character and make her independent, which is more than you or I ever had, not that we didn't strengthen our characters, or at least I did the best I could with mine and circumstances were never too easy, although I don't stand back for anybody today, and I hope you don't either Iris, if you've got half the gumption I tried to drum into you.'

'You say Girlie's back?' I asked weakly, feeling all the gumption I might have had draining out of me.

'Said she couldn't stand it,' Gran said, 'and I wasn't surprised. Told you all along, didn't I?'

'Well, you didn't like the idea anyway,' I reminded her and I began to worry frantically about what we were going to do now.

'What *I* like is beside the point,' Gran said. 'It always is, isn't it? The point is, if she was sent she should have stayed. But you've made a rod for your own back, Iris.'

'So you're always telling me,' I said, and I felt suddenly terribly weary, so weary that when Girlie came in and said 'Hello Mother' with a crooked, apologetic little smile, it was some time before I could say: 'I'll talk to you later.'

'Talk to her!' Gran said. 'You know what she says? She says she is not going back to university at all! Not even the local one!'

I looked at Girlie and I wondered how Gran could miss seeing it. But maybe it was so obvious to me only because I knew, because I was looking for it.

If she refused to go back to the Home I'd have to tell Gran. Or maybe, somehow, I could get Gran to go into a Home? I didn't know. I couldn't think straight any more. But I did know, really, deep inside: it would be easier to try to persuade Girlie, because nothing would ever budge Gran.

Girlie

It was great to be home again, even if home was that poky little flat. When I looked at my tie-dyed lampshade I nearly cried. Not because it was so bad, and it wasn't terribly good, but because it was mine. I tried to explain that to Mother and to make her believe that I'd really tried to like the place, cross my heart, but she was so upset that I had to remind her that she'd crossed her heart too about my leaving if I didn't like it.

I nearly told Gran all about it when she brought me some cocoa. I nearly said: 'Gran, that place, you'd never believe it!' Like I did when I was young, telling her things that had happened at school, only it was never really worth it because she'd just go on and on, rooting away, getting all sorts of other things out of me as well, things that I didn't want her to know. But of course I couldn't tell Gran anything over the cocoa. How could you take a sip of cocoa and say: 'You know, Gran, it wasn't the place itself, or the people individually, it was all of us together like that, too many of us, like a battery of hens waiting to lay their eggs. I couldn't stand it.'

Then I remembered that I couldn't say anything at all because Gran didn't know yet. So I just went on drinking my cocoa, saying nothing.

Mother

I couldn't feel anything any more. I was anaesthetised. I bumped into the passage wall twice on the way to the bedroom and it could have been the gin, but it was more likely the shock of Girlie pitching up like that, landing the whole problem back in my lap.

She closed the door so Gran wouldn't hear us. I wasn't even up to worrying about that any more because if she was back Gran was going to know sooner or later. Everyone was going to know. And after I'd done my best to stop everyone from knowing. At that moment everything was beyond me, even tears.

I asked Girlie: 'Why didn't you stay there?'

'I couldn't stand it,' she said. 'Like being one of a battery of hens about to lay their eggs.'

'Eggs?' I felt stupid, befuddled. I was beginning to think I'd never understand anything any more.

'Well,' she said, 'it *was* like a Finishing School, I suppose. I shared a room, we rapped and listened to the radio. Only there was a girl who wasn't very bright, she kept coming back after she'd had her baby, after they'd taken it away and got a job for her, she kept coming back, looking for it and crying.'

'But you *tried* to like it? You crossed your heart,' I said.

'I promise you,' Girlie said. 'Another thing, most of the girls were having to give up their babies, so they couldn't bear to talk about them. And there was this girl who had a whole layette, everything, nappies and little tiny bootees, only she couldn't keep the baby and she had to go into a mental home straight after because she couldn't cope any more. She wouldn't stop eating and when they put her on a diet she banged her spoon on the table all the time.' Girlie actually lifted her hands to plead with me. 'You see? You understand?'

'All that got you down?' I asked.

'And there was such a hassle,' Girlie said, 'because the girls who couldn't keep their babies wouldn't do the prenatal exercises. They just couldn't bear to be reminded.'

'And you?' I asked her. 'You did yours?'

'Yes,' she said. 'They said it was good for the baby too. Only a lot of them wouldn't do them, they cried a lot, because after doing all that there would be nothing at the end to show for it.'

'So it got you down,' I said, trying to put myself in her place, in the place of all the girls who would go through all that and have nothing at the end to show for it.

'But it wasn't only that,' Girlie said. 'It was the counselling as well.'

'The counselling?'

'This counsellor kept telling me I had a terrible problem. She wouldn't let it be, she said I had to have a problem and she said things about you.'

'About me?' I asked, but I wasn't surprised.

'She kept talking about the unconscious psychological factors. She said I had been rejected by my father and that I was trying to prove my identity and femininity by having a baby. And I said no I'm not. Then she said you felt inferior, you overprotected me and had a sex anxiety and subconsciously that's what drove me into it.'

'Sex anxiety!' I said. 'My God!'

'And all that sort of thing,' Girlie said. 'She just wouldn't let it be. She kept telling me to face up to it. And whenever she talked about, you know ... him, Vern, she called him "the guilty party".' Girlie began to giggle. 'How does that grab you?'

'It's not funny, if that's what you mean,' I said.

'No,' she agreed, 'but she said he was only trying to prove his masculinity in the face of home insecurity and over-mothering. Doesn't *that* grab you?' and she started to giggle again.

'No,' I almost shouted. 'That's probably what it is. His doing this to me, to us.'

'Oh Mother,' Girlie said. 'Now you're talking like *her*.'

I shouldn't have raised my voice because Gran called 'Iris?' before she came in, without even knocking.

'You've upset your mother, that's what you've done,' Gran told Girlie, 'coming back like this. But I was against it from the start, as your mother will recall. There's no place like home, especially for a young gel. Now, there's no need to get into a tizzy Iris, there's no need to shout at her and take on so. I'll make us some cocoa.'

'We've already had cocoa,' Girlie said.

'Sometimes a second cup of cocoa doesn't do a body any harm,' Gran said. 'And I think it's a very good sign, Girlie preferring her own home, just like I said she should. It's only natural when you're a young gel. You should be pleased, Iris.'

'Pleased,' I said, and I got into bed, turning my face to the wall in a gesture I didn't expect Girlie to care about or Gran to understand.

6

Gran

Iris put her newspaper down and looked at me with that funny sneaky look she's got in her eye lately.

'They say here,' she said, 'that loneliness is the biggest tragedy of old age. Even the well off are looking for accommodation in Homes, for security and escape from loneliness.'

'Ah yes,' I said, and I could see what she was up to now. 'Loneliness. Well, at least I'm lucky there. I've got a daughter and a granddaughter. I don't know what loneliness is.'

Iris goes on looking at me, all sneaky, so I went on knitting and nodding my head.

'They're not poor Homes, you know Gran,' she says. 'There are waiting lists today.'

'Ah well, let them wait,' I said, 'the poor souls.'

'They've got physiotherapy, occupational therapy, group work. They do things for themselves and keep busy,' she says.

'That's good,' I said. 'There's nothing like keeping busy. I should know. I did the sheets today and defrosted the fridge, and that reminds me, do you know the butcher's wife finally left him?'

At that Iris suddenly gets all bitter. 'And he doesn't know why, I suppose. Men never do.'

'It gives one something to think about,' I said. 'It keeps one busy. I like to be amongst people and their troubles. I try to help where I can. Just leave her, I said. She'll be back. A woman without a man is like a ship without a sail, I said, and if she cared enough to buy herself a wig ...'

'I don't give a damn about the butcher's wife,' Iris says.

'That's because you're not interested in people,' I told her. 'And that's a mistake. People who are not interested in people end up having a lonely old age, you mark my words.'

But instead of marking my words Iris ups and throws down the paper and flounces off to the bathroom which is no solution to anything. I'm beginning to worry about Iris so when she comes back I say to her:

'You don't know how lucky you are, having your own mother still with you. People don't realise that today. In my day there was always a Gran in the house, sitting on the porch, doing the odd bits and pieces of mending, someone the children could talk to and the mother could say: "Gran, won't you see to the potatoes for me there's a dear, while I get on with the bedrooms?" Little things like that, and boiling the tongue. You and Girlie don't know how lucky you are. I never had a Grannie.' And now I come to think of it, we never even had a porch. But I could see Iris wasn't in the mood to care about things like that.

Mother

I'd never get Gran into a Home, I knew that, and with her and Girlie together like that, I was expecting her to notice any day and when she finally pulled me into the corner next to the fridge and whispered: 'You know, Iris, there's something funny about Girlie,' it was almost a relief.

'Funny?' I asked. That wasn't how I would have described it, but Gran always had her own way of putting things.

'You know, funny,' she said. 'Sort of odd.'

I couldn't stand the suspense so I just plunged straight in, to get it over with. 'Girlie's expecting,' I said, and it sounded terrible, even though I'd had a long time to get used to the idea myself.

'I suspect it's got something to do with that university you sent her to,' Gran whispered.

'That wasn't a university,' I said. 'It was a Home for

Unmarried Mothers.'

'I've always had my doubts about universities for girls, you know that,' Gran said, and there was a long pause while she looked puzzled.

'But tell me,' she said, 'what's this you're saying about a Home? Didn't she go to the university?'

'She's *expecting*, Gran,' I said, and it sounded even worse because of the way Gran was looking.

'Expecting? What?' she asked.

'A *baby*,' I said. 'What else do you expect?' I was being quite brutal but I could see I'd have to be or we would be there, stuck in the corner next to the fridge all night.

'A *baby*!' she said. 'But she's not married! Girlie isn't married ... you never told me ...'

'Please don't be *stupid*, Gran,' I said.

'Stupid?' she asked, in a stupid sort of way and I felt dreadfully sorry for her. 'Well, but I mean, it's the usual thing isn't it? To get married first, isn't it?'

'Yes,' I said. 'It is. But I'm afraid she isn't.'

'She isn't? But you say she's expecting? She isn't married but she's expecting?' Gran moved away slowly and sat down on the kitchen stool. 'But you know, I thought so,' she said. 'I thought there was something funny, but I couldn't put my finger on it. I just said so, didn't I? It was that funny look she had. The other night in the bathroom I said to myself, I'll be blowed if there isn't something funny about that gel, that's what I said. *Expecting*?' Gran looked at me in horror. 'Well, what are you doing about it, Iris?'

'What do you expect me to do?' I asked her. 'Push a knitting needle up her?'

'Ah, but that's vulgar, Iris,' Gran said. 'You're my own daughter but you can be very vulgar. Maybe a woman needs a man just to keep her from getting vulgar.'

'All right,' I said. 'I'm vulgar. That doesn't help. Girlie's ...'

'There's no need to go on saying it,' Gran said. 'It happens in the best of families. It's a terrible shame, but it does happen.

She'll have to get married, that's all. Lots of girls have to get married, it's a terrible shame, but ...'

'To who?' I asked. 'Who is she going to get married to?'

'Who? Don't you be stupid, Iris,' Gran said. 'To the father, of course. She knows who the father is, I hope?'

'She knows,' I told her. 'But he's gone.'

'Gone? Gone where?' Gran asked.

'She doesn't know. For all she knows he might be in Kathmandu, drinking sitar.'

'Drinks too, does he?' Gran said gloomily. 'But he'll have to do, if she's expecting. Get the police after him, Iris.'

'She won't,' I said. 'She says she won't blackmail him.'

'*She* won't,' Gran snorted. 'She isn't twenty-one yet. We're her legal guardians. It's up to us to blackmail him. Just you get him back here.'

'He could be anywhere in the *world*,' I told her. 'I don't even have his proper name.'

'What's she thinking of doing then?' Gran asked.

'Nothing,' I said miserably. 'She says she's going to do nothing.'

'Has *she* got his proper name?' Gran asked.

I shook my head.

'You mean, she didn't even know his *name*?' Gran asked, and it sounded awful, the way she said it.

'She knew him by his nickname,' I said. 'But what does that matter? She refuses to *make* him marry her, just because she's expecting, even if she did know where he was, which she doesn't ...'

'It's that university,' Gran said. 'I told you you shouldn't have ...'

'She wasn't at any university!' I said. 'She was in a Home for Unmarried Mothers!'

'Home for Unmarried Mothers!' Gran said, and I could see she was in a state of shock. 'Well then, what's she doing out of it?'

'She didn't like it.'

'She didn't *like* it! She's an unmarried mother and she's in a Home for Unmarried Mothers and she didn't like it!'

'I know,' I said. 'How do you think I feel?'

'I don't know how *you* feel,' Gran said. 'You can't get hold of his right name, you can't get the police to bring him back and make him marry her, you can't even make her stay where she's out of the sight of respectable people so how do I know how you feel? But I know how *I'm* going to feel, with her walking around expecting and unmarried, so how am I going to talk about the butcher's wife or Esmé McKechnie's grandson when my own granddaughter ...' For a minute I thought Gran was going to cry, but instead she said: 'But I *warned* you Iris, the way you were letting her have her own head ...'

That annoyed me. 'How?' I asked her. 'How was I letting her have her own head?'

'By giving her too much rope,' Gran said. 'I saw it coming, years ago ...'

'No you didn't,' I said. 'Whenever I wanted to pull her up you dragged her on to your lap, come to Gran, Gran's little Girlie ...'

'No, it wasn't,' Gran said. 'And what's wrong with that? A little bit of affection? A little bit of love? Maybe I didn't do it often enough. Maybe that's why she did it. Maybe she was starved for love, the poor gel, but she could have come to me, her own Gran ...' and then the tears started to roll down her cheeks. I hadn't seen Gran cry in years, so I told her: 'It wasn't that. Girlie isn't a baby any more. At least, she's old enough to be having a baby!'

'Dear Lord,' Gran moaned. 'It's the food.'

'What's the food?' I asked, and I thought, she's been precipitated into senility. And no wonder, I was beginning to feel that way myself.

'The vegetables,' she said. 'The stuff they've been putting down to make the vegetables grow, the DDT and things they use to make the chickens lay more eggs, that's at the bottom of it, that's why they grow up too quickly these days, and the stuff they put in the water, the chloride that makes it so flat, we should have been able to give her good clean rain water and this would never have happened, you mark my words, Iris …'

'Oh Gran, for God's sake,' I said.

'And there you go blaspheming again,' she groaned. 'Calling the wrath of the Lord down on us every end and side, no wonder we're being punished now, and what in God's name am I going to tell Esmé McKechnie? Have you thought about that?'

'Look,' I said, 'no one is going to know. Girlie has promised to stay in the flat, she's crossed her heart and if she can't take *that*, she's promised to go straight back to the university, I mean the Home for Unmarried Mothers.'

'But what about sunshine?' Gran wailed, and I thought, it's not just senility, it's unhinged her; and no wonder, I was feeling pretty demented myself.

'What about sunshine?' I asked.

'For that baby's bones,' she said, 'vitamin D.' And I thought, it's all right. As soon as Gran starts making obstacles, she's feeling better, it's all right. So I said: 'The lounge gets the sun every morning. You can make her sit in it if you're worried about the baby's bones.'

'And the African violets?' she asked.

'They'll have to take turns,' I said. 'You'll have to decide which is more important, the African violets or the baby's bones.'

'Ah, but you're a hard woman, Iris,' she said. 'It's not the poor little mite's fault.'

And it wasn't, of course, but I could see just how the poor little mite was going to ruin all our lives. I wasn't really hoping for anything any longer but I couldn't help thinking: if I got what I got with two dependants what chance would I have with three?

7

Girlie

Mother and Gran were so upset and uptight that they made me feel that way too. Mother even asked me: 'If you had to do that, couldn't you have used something?' So I knew how they looked at it: the real sin wasn't making love, it was having a baby, and I couldn't think of anything to say and she gripped my shoulder and said: 'Couldn't you?' and I mumbled we didn't think ... and she said: 'No, of course not, didn't think, behaving like animals, animals don't think either.' That was a terrible thing to say about animals, and I thought no, that's all wrong. It's the other way around, to use something, to fix things, then you'd *really* be behaving like animals, or not even animals, because they take the consequences as part of the natural thing.

But I didn't want to quarrel with her, I didn't want to talk about it much because she was so uptight she'd never understand how it was, how it was like the sun or the rain, it just happened, with no strings, no reservations or restrictions, no should have and what if, but only must, because that was the way it had to be. So I couldn't feel guilty about it, I tried, because I'd grown up thinking about what ifs and should haves, but I couldn't feel guilty. I only felt bad, about Mother and Gran, because they were feeling so bad, and I said I was sorry because I was and I thought that that was what they wanted, that that would help, only I didn't truly regret it, and it didn't help, perhaps because they could see I didn't really regret it.

Maybe that's why they went around looking so bewildered, as if they didn't know where I could have sprung from, as if I didn't belong because I didn't have the same ideas and feelings, and trying to find all sorts of reasons and explanations for what I'd done, and I knew all I had to do was go to them and say I had been deceived, seduced, or raped and they'd understand it then and be happy again and I'd be part of their scene.

But I couldn't do that. I couldn't lie about how it had been with Vern and me, so they went on thinking I was lost or fallen, maybe mad, or whatever it was they thought about girls who did what I did and had a baby and then didn't even have the common decency to be really guilty and sorry about it.

Gran

I thought and I thought and in the end I could only come to one conclusion:

'It's this wearing of jeans,' I told Iris. 'Even to parties. I've been watching all this brew up, ever since she went to that party.'

'What party?' Iris asks.

'That class party,' I told her.

'But that was years ago,' she says.

'Everything has a beginning,' I told her. 'Everything's got to start somewhere. And this business started at that party.'

'Good Lord,' Iris says. 'I couldn't have stopped her from going to her class party. All the other girls...'

'That's not the point,' I said. 'If she had to go to a party she should have been made to wear a nice little frock, like a little lady. I don't mind telling you, Iris,' I said, 'that I was that shocked. When she went in to dress I remember I gave her a little eau de cologne. This will make you smell nice and fresh, I told her, like a little lady. But she didn't use it, oh no, and when she came out of that room she looked just like she went in, in jeans. Her best jeans, she said. But best or worst, that's not and the point. Jeans make the boys think. They give the boys the wrong ideas. And that's where it all started.'

144

'Oh Gran!' Iris says.

'Oh Gran, you say,' I said. 'But I could see it coming all along, only no one ever listens to me. I told you, remember? I asked you, is she going to a party like *that*? And then him, that boy, the father. I warned you about him. His hair's a bit long, I said to you. And what did you say? You said he plays the guitar.'

'And what did *you* say?' Iris asks. 'You said, oh, he's musical then, is he?'

'That's not the point at all,' I told her. 'You as a mother should have made her wear a nice little frock and you should have asked that boy his intentions. In the absence of a father it was up to you to say, if you two are going to walk out together, what are your intentions?'

'But they were only going to see a film. How could I assume he had intentions?'

'Well, as it turns out he had, hadn't he?' I reminded her. 'He had intentions all right.'

'Well, even if I *had* asked him,' Iris says, 'do you think he would have told me? If those were his intentions?'

I had to agree with her there. 'No,' I said, 'but if you had asked him, he would have seen that he had better have the *right* intentions, wouldn't he?'

'But he shouldn't have had *any* intentions,' Iris says, 'with a girl who was barely eighteen!'

'No, but if you had asked him, he would have had to *think* about them, wouldn't he? *That's* the point.'

Iris starts sighing, puffing and blowing like an old horse that's badly winded and I knew just how she felt because that was the way I was feeling too.

'We could go on like this for ever,' she says, 'and it wouldn't change anything now. It wouldn't help.'

'There's still her future to think of,' I reminded her. 'So it does help to find out just where the trouble started. Like with those records, those songs, all about our Lord, jazzed up. I warned Girlie about that. I said, they shouldn't jazz our Lord up and if they do you shouldn't be listening to them. Thin edge of the wedge that was too, oh, I saw it coming, with blasphemy and our Lord all jazzed up and tight jeans, I could see it all.'

'But this isn't the first time it's happening,' Iris says. 'It's always happened, in your day and mine, even without jeans and jazz and it isn't jazz anyway, it's rock, but it still happened!'

'That doesn't make it right,' I told her, 'whether you call it jazz or rock.' But Iris always gets out of arguments by splitting hairs. It's the slippery sort of way of arguing that her father had. But at least she had a father, and that brought me right back to the predicament Girlie was in with her poor fatherless mite and I had to start sighing along with Iris.

8

Mother

Although I didn't say anything I was grateful to Gran. She was scratching around looking for causes, blaming anything and everything, but she didn't really blame me, she didn't mention the divorce, not once. She made a few remarks about women without men, but she didn't once say, child from a broken home ... like all the experts at the Homes had done, rubbing it in, and I was grateful because I was feeling bad enough as it was. I kept thinking, child from a broken home, divorced mother, what could you expect? Because it was a well-known fact, the papers were always full of it, juvenile delinquency and all the rest of it, all children from broken homes, smoking pot, free love and getting themselves into trouble, and I thought maybe this wouldn't have happened if I'd stayed with Frank, and then I thought, no, that's not true, I didn't leave Frank, he left me. There wasn't anything I could do about it. And then I had to go over the whole thing again, how it was, why he'd left me, because I had to see if I was to blame in some way and I tried to remember how it was and the thing that had really struck me, that stuck in my mind, was how pale he'd got, as if that had anything to do with it, but that was what stuck in my mind, his paleness and how he seemed to get paler by the year, by the month, as though all the colour, what there ever was of it, in his looks and his personality, was fading away.

At first if I made him angry he used to get a bit red in the face, but later he didn't even do that, he just stayed pale. When we got married, I remember, his hair was blonde but it turned the colour of ash, or the lack of the colour of ash. And his eyes that had been blue faded too, like overbleached laundry. His hands were beautiful, though, I remember, with beautifully shaped pale pink nails, but they went white as well. Even his clothes seemed to fade and he began to look like a watercolour that had been left out in the rain. I remember towards the end I could hardly touch him, I was scared my hand would go right through, he didn't look solid any more. It got on my nerves, it really upset me and sometimes I thought I could sweep him out, like dust, or fluff.

I thought, maybe he's got TB. Gran thought he was ill too and then she started in with her poultices. Only he didn't have any sprains, bruises, headaches, ulcers on the skin or sore throats so there wasn't anywhere, really, to put a poultice.

'Try his head,' I told her, but on thinking back that wasn't funny.

Gran was dead serious about fixing him up though, and Girlie said that between us we would finish him off. Gran and I laughed, I remember, but now that didn't seem funny any more either.

Frank knew Gran meant well but he wouldn't have anything to do with the poultices. She made one of mashed raw onions which made the whole house stink for days but when she wanted to put it on the soles of his feet he wouldn't let her. He didn't say anything, he just stood up and wouldn't sit down or lie down until she'd taken it away. Of course it was ridiculous, but Gran was really trying to help. And Frank was lucky that it was only raw onion, because she told me about another one made with pig's lard spread on a piece of brown paper and sprinkled with sulphur.

Just before he left I remember Frank spent all his time lying on his bed staring at the ceiling, sometimes not even getting undressed at night to get into bed, with his arms folded behind his head and not answering us when we spoke to him, taking no notice of us at all, just acting as though we weren't there, and then Gran started talking about the atmosphere in the room. I thought she meant the emotional atmosphere which wasn't even an atmosphere it was so negative, but she was talking about the air and she put some eau de cologne in a bowl and put a match to it, right next to Frank's head.

'You'll find this refreshing,' she said.

I'll never forget it. Frank took no notice when she came in with the bowl but when the eau de cologne burst into flames he turned and looked at her. It was an awful haunted sort of look and I really began to worry about him. I began to think maybe he was depressed about something, but I didn't know what he'd got to be so depressed about. And he wouldn't see a doctor. He wouldn't even answer me when I suggested it. Maybe the burning of that eau de cologne was the last straw, although he didn't say anything, because not long after that he left.

Gran thought he was ungrateful and Girlie cried for a time, but I couldn't feel anything very much because it seemed to me that he hadn't really been there for a long time, the way his personality had faded, and his looks.

I know now he must have been ill or depressed, and if he'd asked me to help him I would have tried. But he didn't. He just cut me off. I must have resented that because I let Gran in with that eau de cologne just to see if it wouldn't shake him up a bit, maybe even make him laugh. But it didn't. It just made him give her that haunted look.

There wasn't anything more I could have done, about Frank, or preventing a divorce after he had deserted, and I began thinking about Girlie again. She was Frank's daughter too. I had to take that into account. But there was nothing very queer about her. She did get that odd faraway look in her eyes but all the young people were looking like that these days. It was the fashion, being other-worldly, or something.

I didn't think there was any way to explain it, any of it, although Gran would go on trying, and I suppose I would too.

Gran

I was still trying to make some sense of the whole sorry affair, so I said to Iris: 'It's all those couples making love like that all over TV.'

'But that's overseas,' Iris says. She always has to take everything I say at its face value.

'I know,' I said, 'but that's not the point. It's the principle of the thing. If something like this can happen to Girlie when we haven't even got that can you imagine what's going to happen when we do get it?'

Iris shook her head and I have to admit I couldn't imagine it either. I couldn't imagine anything worse happening than what was happening to Girlie.

'And the nudes in the dirty magazines all over Rome that even the Pope was complaining about.'

'But that's Italy,' Iris says.

'Yes,' I said, 'that's Italy, but what about that house in Johannesburg where they found all those bottles and empty pill boxes and underwear? It's going on all over the world, it's the way the world's going and I really don't know what it's coming to.' But I did know that soon there would be no room in it any more, not for people like me with some morals, and maybe Iris.

'It's the whole break-up of family life,' I said.

Iris's head jerks up and she says, quick off the mark like she always is when I've touched a sore spot:

'I was wondering when you were going to start blaming me. But you weren't exactly against the divorce at the time, if I remember.'

'I wasn't meaning that,' I told her. 'What could you do if you were deserted? And at least you had the good sense to marry him *before* he deserted you. Which is more than Girlie had.'

'Well, when he played golf all weekend you were the one who advised me to pack his clothes and leave them in the hall so that he could get out as soon as he got back. Maybe I should have compromised a little.'

'Oh, maybe this, maybe that,' I said. 'I'm your mother. I didn't like to see you unhappy.'

'Well, you're still seeing me,' Iris said, 'unhappy.'

I felt really sorry for her. 'Now then,' I said, 'you'll not want to be blaming yourself too much,' and just then Girlie comes in and asks why someone has got to be blamed. I'm beginning to think she has got no proper sense of shame, that gel hasn't. It's like she was born with a part missing, maimed or crippled somewhere in her morals.

'Well, I'll tell you,' I told her, 'who's really to blame. It's him. That boy who led you astray and then saw fit to leave you to face the consequences alone. He's the one to blame, with his beard and his bell and his old tyre sandals!'

'I'm not blaming him,' Girlie says, pert as you please, 'nor anyone else.' Like I said, she must be maimed or crippled somewhere, maybe in her conscience.

'Anyway,' I said to Iris, because I was feeling really sorry for her, 'the Lord moves in some mysterious ways and everything's a blessing in disguise if you have the faith to look for it. Look at Emily, for instance.'

'Emily?' Iris asks. 'What's Emily got to do with it?' She never gives me a chance to finish, before she's jumping in, contradicting me.

'Well,' I said, 'if Emily hadn't got those lumps she'd be here right now and the whole location would know all about Girlie, not to mention Esmé McKechnie.'

'You think it's a blessing in disguise?' Iris sneers. 'Emily wanted a baby and couldn't, but Girlie's having one?'

'Well, it's not an unmixed blessing,' I had to admit. 'For one thing I'll not be able to have anyone else in to help me around the flat, in case they talk.'

'Girlie can help you,' Iris says, 'she may be expecting but she's not paralysed!' And I could see that she was really feeling bitter just then, so bitter that she wouldn't be able to see that anything was a blessing in disguise. But you've got to believe it. You've got to go on believing it if you don't want to go off your head sometimes.

Girlie

I went to bed and left them to go on arguing about whose fault it was because they had to have that, they had to have someone to blame especially when there wasn't anyone, and I thought, of course I'll help Gran in the flat, I'm not paralysed, although Mother needn't have said it like that, and then I remembered the crippled student Vern had told me about, who was marching with a few others. Some of them had just been standing around but they started running to catch up when they saw him, until the march had grown to fifty, a hundred of them, in a long straggly column, and this guy hobbling along with one foot swinging in a heavy black boot and his shoulders all crooked and hunched up over his crutches.

'What's bugging you man?' Vern asked him. 'Where are you heading?'

He looked at Vern and his face was white and sweat was beginning to run into his eyes but he couldn't wipe it away and he said: 'John Vorster Square.' Vern told him that was miles away and he said: I'll get there.'

That really grabbed Vern and he asked why, what was bugging them all, and the crippled guy said:

'The lot, man, the lot.'

He had to stop for a while to get his breath, leaning on one crutch and holding the other in his armpit so he could wipe his face, and Vern said: 'You're crazy man,' because he had started up again, and his breath, he was just gasping, trying to catch up, with his foot swinging like that.

'Let me help you,' Vern said, because it was beginning to bug him, this guy half killing himself like that to protest, but he said no, he had to do it, he had to march, so Vern stayed with him in case he collapsed and he said the crazy thing was that they didn't show anybody anything, not even the crippled guy who had nearly killed himself just getting there because when they got there they all got arrested and herded into a compound because they didn't have a permit to stage any kind of protest march about anything. Vern nearly got shoved in with them until the crippled guy said no, he's not marching, he's an innocent bystander, and Vern said he didn't know how he'd even been able to say that because his face was all twisted with pain.

Vern thought he could rap with him, really rap, because for most of the rest of them it was a bit of a gas, mixing it with the fuzz, he didn't think they cared so much about injustices and all that, because when a bearded guy looked down from one of the cells they started yelling at him, 'What you in for?' and when he laughed his stoned head off and said: 'Pot man, pot,' they thought it was great.

The fuzz took names, pictures and fingerprints, Vern said, and sent them home like naughty children and Vern knew it wasn't going to count for a thing, and maybe the crippled guy knew it too, because when he got out he just went to sit on the pavement with his crutches lying in the gutter and Vern sat down next to him and told him:

'You made it, man, you got here.'

And when the crippled guy shook his head, Vern said: 'That counts for something, man.' But he just went on shaking his head, so Vern said: 'It'll count for you.' But Vern could see that wasn't enough because his head still hung right down, between his knees, and he said:

'I didn't do it for me.'

'That's what counts,' Vern told him. 'That's the only thing that really counts.'

But it wasn't enough for the crippled guy. He hunched his shoulders back over his crutches and swung off. Vern knew why too, just like he did. Because the injustices were still there.

So if Mother and Gran could think about that for a bit, who're they going to blame?

9

Mother

I was still thinking, even if it was true that the divorce had done something to Girlie, warped her, stopped her from adjusting properly or something, what could I have done about it?

Frank didn't even show up at the hearing and I'd had to tell the judge he'd just walked out. He hadn't been interested in the marriage, much, and he wasn't interested in the divorce, so what could I have done about it?

By that time I was sick anyway, right down to the pit of my stomach, but the judge wouldn't give up, he kept telling me how many marriages he had patched up, at the eleventh hour, right from the bench, and if my husband was so uncooperative as not to appear for the eleventh hour patching up there had to be a reason and he wanted it, from me.

Only I couldn't give him one because I didn't know myself. It would have sounded silly to say my husband sort of faded away, so I said I didn't know and I could see he thought I was lying, but he went on trying to help me and I answered the questions to get it over with because I felt really sick to my stomach. Getting a divorce takes it out of you. I told him we didn't have any quarrels but I couldn't say: maybe if we did have them at least I would have known Frank was alive, because then he'd have asked me to explain and I didn't understand myself, I just kept thinking of that eau de cologne but I couldn't have told him about that either.

Then he asked, was Frank interested in someone else? And I had to say I didn't know again and I almost said I wished there had been because then at least I'd have had something to fight, some reason I could understand.

Then he read me a little lecture about physical love and how if that was all it should have been little faults and failings

154

would have gone unnoticed and forgiven. I nearly told him Frank didn't really have any faults because he hardly did or said anything, before I realised he was meaning me, that maybe I had the faults that Frank couldn't forgive because the physical side wasn't what it should have been, and I just got tired of the whole business, wanting to get it over with, but he went on and on about the magnification of small grievances to be stored up as ammunition for the next outburst if *that* sphere of the relationship was unsatisfactory and I didn't bother to tell him that there weren't any outbursts, that that was what was wrong and queer about the whole thing, so he went on and on about thermometers to measure the conversational temperature between husband and wife and I was feeling so sick I had to end it so I said for a long time there hadn't been any conversational temperature to measure, to speak of, and it sounded so funny I had to giggle a bit and he looked very disapproving and asked:

'Well then, were you surprised when your husband left you?' And I said, 'Yes,' because that was the truth, I really hadn't thought that Frank was up to making a decision like that and seeing it through; but that judge would never have understood that some things are sick and just slowly die and there doesn't have to be anything dramatic like adultery, or assault, although I suppose in a way eau de cologne bursting into flames next to one's head is quite dramatic.

Anyway there wasn't anything I could do about it. Frank ignored the restitution order, just as I knew he would, leaving me with Girlie who must have been warped in some way by the whole business, although I hadn't noticed it before. And there was nothing I could do, not now, it was too late, and I started feeling sick again, right down to the pit of my stomach, and I couldn't have giggled about anything then, if there had been anything to giggle about.

Gran

Barefaced, that's what we would have called it. The worst I ever did was steal a few apples and then I felt guilty about it for months afterwards, afraid I'd get sent to hell.

Lack of communication with the young, the newspapers call it. The generation gap. But the gap isn't on *our* side, it's *them* who don't want to communicate. Girlie wasn't interested in communicating with me. I could see that.

Iris was nearly as bad when she was that age, teenagers they called them. Well, there weren't any of them around when I was a gel and we never missed it. But I never let lack of communication or any gap stop me with Iris and at least she's got a healthy sense of shame and guilt to show for it which is more than Girlie has when she's expecting a child without a father and no one doing anything about it that I could see so it was up to me as usual to sort things out, because Iris wasn't getting anywhere. It's a state of shock, she says, but Girlie'd had nearly eight months to get over the shock. I'd managed to get over mine and everyone knows a pregnancy like this is always worse for the kinfolk, like those who are left behind in a bereavement.

She wasn't shocked, not as far as I could see. She was smug. Getting fat like a cat, sitting daydreaming and licking her chops and preening herself in front of the mirror. I caught her at that, looking to see how big she's getting as if that's something to be proud of in her situation. No shame at all she hasn't, taking everything for granted like that, Iris'll work for her and the baby, because she's got this idea she's keeping it. The gel's not been made to *think*.

She was supposed to be helping around the flat, to get some exercise instead of lounging around all the time, because the baby needed some circulation, so she was pushing a cloth along the tops of the furniture, leaving rings of dust around all the ornaments, but I decided I'd talk to her about that later.

I took up my knitting and settled myself down.

'Girlie,' I said, 'leave that for a moment and we'll have a little heart-to-heart. It's been such a long time since you came to tell me all your little troubles like that time you were crying because ...' but that was so long ago I couldn't remember it myself. 'Well that's beside the point. The point is, who did you come to but your old Gran, and didn't your Gran always try to teach you the right and proper thing and see that you got to Sunday School on time and went to church or you would never even have got confirmed?'

Girlie stood leaning on the duster and looking at me so at least she must have been listening for a change.

'Well now,' I said, 'You've made a terrible mistake. I'm not judging you, I'm not saying anything, but there it is, you can't get away from the facts. Now, we all pay for our mistakes. It wouldn't be fair if you got away with it, without paying something, and believe me, if I could pay for you, if my lifeblood could do it ...'

She wandered around to look closely into my face. 'What's bugging you, Gran?' she asked me, pert as you please.

I made up my mind to come straight to the point. But it was very difficult, talking to Girlie these days.

'What's bugging me,' I said, using her awful slang to help the communication between us and close the gap a bit, 'is what should be bugging *you*. You've got hold of this idea from somewhere that you can keep the baby with never a thought for your mother and me, oh yes, with your mother to support it and me to look after it when you go off back to the university or looking for work, and no father; well, never mind about your mother and me, don't consider us, but that poor little mite needs a home and a decent respectable life where no one can point a finger at it, so it will have a surname and all the advantages, you've got to think about what's good for the baby, this isn't Hollywood, you know.'

Girlie's shoulders began to shake and I thought, ah yes, now you've been made to think; let her cry for a while, it'll do her good, and then we'll have a nice cup of tea, with the air clear between us.

But then I saw she wasn't crying, she was snorting and snuffling, and I thought no, she can't be *laughing*. She must have gone hysterical, I thought, because she burbled and bubbled and laughed out loud, collapsing on to the settee with her legs up in the air and her skirt up around her waist, and I remember thinking again, even then, at least she can't wear jeans any more. That's one blessing in disguise.

'Oh Gran!' she was shrieking, 'Hollywood!'

Oh Gran, I thought, yes, oh Gran. And I could have got hold of her then and there and given her a good sound slap.

'Sorry,' she was gasping, 'I'm sorry, only it's so funny!'

'Oh,' I said, 'funny, is it? You'll want to remember that this time you haven't landed with your backside in butter. You'll find out soon enough how funny it is.'

'My backside in butter!' she burbled.

She was getting me properly riled up this time. She was beyond shame, I could see that, and she was putting my blood pressure up too, I could feel it ringing in my ears and my face getting hot.

'You'll be giving me a stroke next,' I warned her.

She pulled herself together then and came over, to put her arm around my shoulders and her cheek on my head, and the disgrace that was her stomach right in front of my face. 'I'm sorry, Gran,' she said. 'Really.'

That didn't help my blood pressure much and I took to wondering: where was her sense of shame? It was unhealthy, it wasn't normal. Every normal gel has a sense of shame. But it was missing in her. I didn't know who she took after, just like I didn't know what the world was coming to. The only thing I did know was that there was no point in trying to talk to Girlie any more.

Girlie

I knew everything would be all right with Gran and Mother if I got married, even at the very last minute. It wouldn't be such a sin then. But Vern didn't think much of marriage and I wasn't sure either. Mother's didn't work out, although they must have thought it would, her and Dad. But they were never together, like Vern and I were. They never understood each other, like I understood Vern even when I didn't know what he was talking about. When he was on about life being antithetical with its paradoxes, the rational and the more important non-rational, and all the current anti's, I didn't understand, really, until it came in a flash, like when he said: 'It's a beginning, isn't it, to admit that no one can know where to begin?' I understood that, and he knew, and it was a close sort of feeling, so maybe it would work better with Vern and me. We weren't always pulling apart like Mother and Dad were.

I remember how sad Dad used to look and I felt so sorry for him, but he expected me to side with Mother and Mother expected that too and a child can't always fight that sort of expectation.

Vern never expected anything from anybody, but then he didn't expect anybody to expect anything from him either. He was hooked on freedom and that guru Krishna-someone who disbanded all his followers because they wanted something from him that he couldn't give, a pattern of the whole truth; because, Vern said, truth was a pathless land. There were maps, but no one map.

I often thought Dad expected something from me. He used to watch me as though he wanted something but I didn't know what it was. He didn't say anything and I didn't know what to say.

Maybe it was easier to talk to Vern because he didn't want anything from me except what I wanted to give him. He said all evil sprang from demands, and demands were always the result of self-concern.

I wasn't as selfless as Vern. I had it in me to demand; I did want him, himself, his whole self, every part of him, down to his warm dry hands.

When I was small and Dad used to hold my hand his hands were so cold and clammy I couldn't stand it. But his mouth was always dry. His tongue and lips were all dry and cracked, like the bottom of a dam in a drought.

And he could never make up his mind, he couldn't decide about anything. He would pretend to be deciding but he was really only waiting for Mother, or Gran, to decide. Maybe if I had the chance now I could think of something to say to him. But it was too late. It was probably too late even before he left. And he had to leave, I think, for the same reasons Vern did, even if he didn't know them. He had to be free and alone, like Vern, and that meant having to go, like Vern, to find some space to be free and alone in.

Maybe I could talk to Dad about all that now. I think I was beginning to understand him.

Mother

'Well, I'm afraid we'll have to face up to it,' Gran said as soon as I came into the kitchen.

I was so exhausted, so dispirited I couldn't face up to anything more and it was only through sheer force of habit that I was able to ask: 'What now?'

'I'm afraid she's out of her mind,' Gran said.

I knew, somehow, that she wasn't talking about the butcher's wife, or Emily or even Esmé McKechnie, so I sighed and asked, just to get it over with: 'What's she done now?'

Gran pursed her lips and her eyes swivelled around, and I thought, sometimes she looks just like those cut-out cats Girlie used to bring home from school, but even that didn't make me feel like smiling.

'She says she's keeping the baby,' Gran said. 'Out of her mind, that gel is. Not married and talking about keeping the baby. Are you out of your mind, I asked her, when you're not decently married? And you know what she does? She laughs. Laughs! And who's going to support the baby *and* you? I asked her. Your poor mother who's got enough on her plate as it is? But she'll support the baby herself, she says. And I suppose I'll have to mind it, I asked her. I'm getting a bit old for that sort of lark, I told her. But no, she'll get a nanny, she says. So when you're out working and she's out working there'll be me and the baby and the nanny in here getting on each other's nerves. She's out of her mind, of course. It's happened before that they go out of their minds, carrying babies that have no fathers; for all we know, that poor little mite already knows that it's got no father …'

'I know,' I sighed, 'I know all about it,' and I started to shell the peas for Gran, just for something to do, concentrating on the sharp juicy crack of the pods and the peas as they pinged into the bowl.

'Your daughter's out of her mind and all you can say is that you know!' Gran said. 'You're a proper ostrich, Iris, you've always had your head in the sand!'

I gritted my teeth and squashed a whole pod of peas. Sometimes I feel I could cheerfully murder Gran. And then I wondered if Girlie ever felt that way about me, that she could cheerfully murder me. And what if we did? What if I cheerfully murdered Gran and Girlie cheerfully murdered me and Girlie's baby cheerfully murdered her when it was old enough? I was feeling really desolate.

'I'll talk to her,' I told Gran, but I went on shelling the peas.

'Talk?' Gran said, with that snorting bray of hers.

That's how it is, I thought. My mother braying like a mule and my daughter swelling up like a dead donkey. Well, hee-haw …

I must have hee-hawed out loud by mistake because Gran

cocked her ear at me. I'd never noticed it before but Gran had very hairy ears, really coarsely haired ears, like a donkey's, only smaller.

'What was that?' she asked.

'I said, hee-haw!' I said, and I thought, put that in your eau de cologne bottle and sniff it.

'You're out of your mind,' Gran said. 'Just like her. Your daughter's got herself into trouble and you stand there neighing like a horse. It's a wonder that I've managed to keep my wits about me with the pair of you around.'

I finished the peas. 'What's she doing now?' I asked.

'Feeling the baby kick,' Gran said. 'That's what she said. It was the baby's kicking that decided her, she said, to keep it, because it was alive and kicking so she couldn't just give it away like that. She's out of her mind. All babies kick. Nothing special about that.'

But there is, I thought as I went through to the bedroom, when it's your baby that's kicking. Only in the circumstances I couldn't say that to her, not even casually.

I felt awfully weary and old as I sat on the bed next to Girlie, like most women do, I suppose, when they're about to become grandmothers, moving suddenly into the next generation.

'Now we've already had this out, Girlie,' I said to her. 'How can you possibly keep it? It won't have a father, it'll grow up with a stigma attached to it.'

I noticed that her eyes had become very soft and moist lately, like a cow's. We're a proper menagerie, I thought, Gran and Girlie and me. 'I can't help it,' she mumbled. 'I love it.'

'You love it,' I said, trying to be firm, cruel to be kind as Gran would have put it. 'Of course. But how much? Enough to do what's best for it?' And I thought, it's easy to talk like this. I hadn't had to give up my baby, that same Girlie who was sitting there now. And I wondered whether it might have been better for her if I had, if she'd grown up in a happier, unbroken home, even if it was a foster home, and now, would she go through my agony one day, wondering if it would have been better for her child if she'd given it up?

'You're so young yet, Girlie,' I told her. 'You'll get married, you'll have other children. But the chances of getting married when you're saddled with a fatherless baby … well. Or *is* he coming back? Will he marry you when he knows? Is that why you …'

'No,' she said. 'I don't know.'

I tried to see, from the expression on her face, whether she really didn't know, or whether she had some hope, for herself and the baby, or if she was pretending, holding out some hope to me, to get me to help her to keep the baby, but I couldn't see anything, or at least not that much from her expression which was simply dumb and obstinate, and uncannily like Frank's used to be.

'You swear you're not in touch with him?' I asked her. 'Cross your heart?'

'Cross my heart,' she said.

'If he doesn't come back,' I said, 'you'll give up the baby?'

And she said 'No,' very quietly, with just that degree of immovable determination in her voice that Frank had had when he'd told me he was leaving. It was eerie and I actually felt the hair prickle at the back of my neck.

Gran

There are some things you can't talk about, especially not to people like Esmé McKechnie, even though she knows what trouble is herself, so when I met her on the stairs all I said was: 'Isn't it terrible, all these actresses having babies without husbands? They're setting this bad example.'

'It just goes to show,' Esmé said.

'Show what?' I asked, because I thought: she's a Catholic, maybe she knows.

'All this long hair and drugs,' she said, 'and overseas in

that show they were sticking their bare backsides and worse out at the audience. And even here, up in Johannesburg, did you read about it? The young people are all sleeping with everybody else and one thirteen-year-old girl was passing VD on to I don't know how many boys. I blame the parents. It's because they don't care any more.'

That wasn't true. It wasn't true that Iris and I didn't care, so I said: 'You can't blame the poor parents for everything. What about young Patrick? You're not blaming Nova ...'

'Oh yes,' she said. 'I blame Nova fair and square. It's bad potty-training, that's what they told her at the clinic and I could have told her that myself. These things always go right back to childhood, but she'd never take any advice from me.'

Bad potty-training. Well, I didn't know. From what I remembered we didn't have any trouble with Girlie that could account for it. She had a bit of bother teething, but she sat on the potty and performed like a little angel right from the start, as far as I could remember.

'Well, I don't know,' I said. 'The way things are going, with all those actresses and hippies, people are not bothering to get married any more.'

'Well, I won't be here to see it come to that,' Esmé said. 'Thanks to the Blessed Virgin.'

I didn't know too much about the Blessed Virgin but I was glad I wouldn't be around to see it happening wholesale either, because it would be a sad day for women and children if men didn't marry them any more.

It was funny in a way and I nearly told Esmé: here's Girlie needing to get married and not wanting to and Iris not needing it and wanting to, but all I said was: 'It's a queer upside-down world and the less I see of it the better because you can't make any sense out of it, that's why I'm glad we haven't got TV, although it's supposed to be so nice for the elderly folk.'

'Talking about elderly folk,' Esmé said, 'Mrs Merriman has found a new char. She's been round to me, do you want her too?'

And I had to say no, I'm managing, which I wasn't really, going down on my knees at my age, but what else could I do unless I wanted everyone to know about Girlie?

'You're doing the floors,' Esmé said, 'and the ironing?'

'We're sending out to the laundry now,' I said. 'And Iris has got me a wax-boy. Pinching a bit, you know, for Girlie to be in residence at the university.'

May the Lord forgive me for all the lies I was having to tell, putting my eternal soul in danger, but what else could I do? I'd already told them all that Girlie had gone to the university in Cape Town, and how could I tell them now what place it really was, and not only what place it really was, but that she hadn't even had the decency to stay there?

10

Girlie

It didn't bug me too much, being shut up in the flat all the time. I could get away by sitting still and thinking about Vern, which took me to where he might be now, one of the places he'd told me about, where the earth was dark-red and the poinsettias and jacarandas grew wild at the side of the road and all the small quiet towns had red brick railway cottages, spired churches, little spaced matchbox African townships and cemeteries with cypresses on the outskirts, all a dusty red-brown. And even the new motels and roadhouses, painted up like rainbows, looked somehow the same which gave him a terrific sense of déjà vu.

I remember Vern telling me that just outside one of those small towns he saw a shake-down shelter, just a bit of canvas spread over a branch between two trees with some box wood and an old tyre, and there were seven Africans, dusty like the town, waiting for the porridge that was cooking over the fire. Vern said hello and they said hello, so he squatted down with them and the Bossboy told him they were clearing the bush for a building site, on contract, for R10 a month and porridge for breakfast and lunch. They were supposed to go into a hostel but it was full and they were freezing to death under the piece of canvas and they had to knock on doors in the town for water.

Vern said they were really bitter about that shelter, the cold, the porridge and having to beg for water. He'd lived like that too, when he'd run out of bread and nobody would give him a job because they thought he was a hippy, but that was the way he'd chosen, so he wasn't bitter, he was happy, he was doing his thing.

But he could see that if you *had* to live on porridge and R10 a month and sleep cold maybe you'd really get turned on by the thought of champagne and oysters or even just a good thick stew.

He wanted to find out, he needed a job then anyway, so he decided to stay, to see what it was like for them, having to work and live on porridge and freezing at night so when the white boss came Vern asked him to put him on contract too, only the boss thought he was joking, or having him on, but when he realised Vern was serious he called him a tramp and a ducktail and a white kaffir so he had to split because he's a pacifist and it looked like the white boss was going to get violent if he didn't. But he'd been sorry to miss that chance. Vern was like that.

Mother

She was going to keep the baby, I could see that, and if I tried to force her, if I *could* force her, she'd never forgive me, I'd lose her, I could see that too. It really was the bitter end. I felt like death, and it didn't help much, Gran feeling that way too and saying it over and over again: 'This is going to be the death of me, Iris.'

Not that I didn't believe it, feeling that way myself, but Gran never can keep things simple.

'When I'm finally going,' she said to me, 'I don't want them to plug me into any machines.'

I didn't get that so I said nothing, but Gran is like a bulldog, it must be her English blood.

'You must promise me, Iris,' she said.

'Promise you what?' I asked, and I thought this business is surely affecting her mind, which didn't surprise me, the way it was affecting mine too.

'When I'm dying,' she said, 'you've got to stop them from plugging me into any machines.'

'Plug you into machines?' I asked, and I thought: my God, a senile dependant, an immoral dependant and an illegitimate dependant, how would that look in the column if I ever felt up to the column again.

Gran pointed at the newspaper. 'Like they say here,' she said. 'Heart-lung machines, kidney machines, blood transfusions, intravenous feedings and all sorts and shapes of tubes and tapes. They say it's arrested death, not life. I'm ready to go when my time comes and if this isn't going to be my time, before my time, then I don't know, but it happens to all of us sooner or later only with me I can feel it's going to be sooner, so I want you to promise me, Iris.'

'Don't be so morbid, Gran,' I told her. 'In any case if I don't sign they might have me up for murder.'

Gran hadn't thought of that because she started plucking at the hairs of her mole. 'That's a terrible thing,' she said, 'if you can't go with dignity today without your relatives being had up for murder.'

'Yes,' I said. 'Well, I don't know,' because I had so much on my mind just then and I was so confused that I thought, why cross my bridge or my eggs before they're hatched, I'll face the tapes and the tubes when I come to them.

Another time it might have been funny and we would have ended up laughing, Gran and I, only now we were too depressed, Gran even more than me, although Girlie was only her granddaughter.

Gran

I tried to make a bit of lemon curd but the eggs aren't what they used to be either. Nothing is like it used to be. You can't even die like you used to die. I could see Iris wasn't really interested in the subject, but then she isn't as close to dying as I am, and the more I thought about it the more it struck me as a terrible thing. Those people who let themselves be plugged into tapes and tubes must be afraid of death, and why? Because they've lost their belief. No one who has belief and faith is afraid of death. That's what's missing today, belief and faith. They can get to the moon all right, as I told Esmé McKechnie, walking out alone amongst those craters, but what if something came crawling out of one of them? That would put the fear of the Almighty into them soon enough.

And Iris can say what she pleases but I believe that if Girlie had been kept in a proper fear of the Almighty she wouldn't be in the predicament she's in. It just made me so sad to think about it, when I thought about how I taught her to pray when she was just a little thing, Gentle Jesus meek and mild … It just made me so mad to see her sitting there without one single thought in her empty head about her future life, let alone life after death, that I said to her:

'If you don't wear shoes in your condition you're going to end up with piles.'

'Oh, I've got them,' she says, all unconcerned. 'Dr Shaw said it's the pressure, the last time he came around.'

'Pressure!' I said. 'It's more like walking around without any shoes on.'

'I always wore shoes,' Iris chips in, 'with Girlie, and I got them just the same.'

'Good thing too,' I said. 'Sensible.' But it annoyed me, Iris always contradicting me like that, and look where it's got her, an unmarried mother for a daughter. 'Pity you didn't take my advice about hanging on to your faith, too.' At that Iris usually shuts up. It's a sore point with her, religion.

'And you,' I said to Girlie, 'the same goes for you.' She didn't answer, so I said: 'Here, you haven't got something wrong with your jaw, have you? Or your tongue?'

They got up to go to bed then, but I saw them give each other that look they give each other when they know I'm right and they haven't got an answer. I sat on for a while. I didn't want them to know they'd upset me, the way they never take my advice, but perhaps I was just generally upset at that time, although I have got my faith that will see me through, which is more than Iris and Girlie have got, and I began to think, maybe it's my fault they've lost their faith like that, maybe I haven't been setting a good enough example, and that upset me even more, so I went to bed too, but I was so upset I couldn't sleep.

I just lay there thinking, about Girlie who had no sense of shame, and Iris who's my own daughter unless they did a switch on me in the hospital and that's been known to happen, but Iris only spoilt Girlie a little bit perhaps, making a rod for her own back as I warned her and now she's got to reap what she sowed, but I didn't really blame her with the gel having no father either, and I couldn't blame her for *that*, although in some ways Frank was a better husband than I ever had, at least he didn't sit on the stoep all the time eating cheese with his penknife and gums when he had a perfectly good set of teeth in a box in the bathroom.

But Iris was a good gel, she never gave me any trouble except for sticking film stars on the walls and leaving all those dirty sticky marks, but she was thrifty, I remember, separating her tissues to make them go twice as far and wearing that white bunny wool jersey until it went yellow although that could have been because it made her bust look bigger.

No, the only thing I really had against Iris was writing to those bleeding hearts men, and then I started thinking, maybe that's where the trouble lies, so I had to get up then and call her into the kitchen, because I believe in being straight and getting things over with so I can get some sleep, and I said to her:

'Maybe that's why Girlie's got herself into trouble, Iris, you writing to those bleeding hearts instead of having a few heart-to-hearts with her, that's your own daughter, if you knew she'd got to an awkward age,' and she said:

'They're not bleeding hearts, they're lonely hearts, and I'm not writing any more,' all in that dead sort of voice she's using these days. She didn't even mind that I'd woken her up.

'Oh,' I said. I wondered what the difference was, but I let that go, because it worried me, the way Iris's voice has gone all dead, and she always was a bit of a nit-picker.

'And why's that?' I asked her, and I thought in a way it's another bad sign, dead voice, dead heart.

'I've lost interest, that's all,' she says.

'Hmmmmm,' I said, and 'no wonder,' I said, but I went back to bed because we couldn't really discuss anything with any enjoyment any more, Iris and me; the spice had gone out of everything, what with the worry about Girlie, and we weren't more than half-hearted about anything and I couldn't help thinking, I just don't understand how God's mind works. Emily couldn't have a baby and she was nearly forty and wanting one and Girlie's only eighteen and having a baby nobody wants, except her. I know we need white babies in this country more than black babies, but why did God let it happen to Girlie when she wasn't even married?

I was having a hard time of it, holding on to my own faith just then. Even when I was praying I kept on wanting to ask, why? But that would have been disrespectful and I didn't want to call God's wrath down on our heads any more than it already was.

Girlie

The book said he'd be starting to suck his thumb and that really grabbed me. I wanted to tell them, I wanted to say, he's sucking his thumb already, he's a real baby, he's even got fingernails and he's about fourteen inches long, that's big enough to hold, and I just know he's got a lot of fine hair like Vern, but I couldn't, not the way they were walking around as if there was a death in the flat instead of a beautiful new life.

I went on trying to meditate and breathe properly so I could lose all self-concern and stop feeling how unfair it was that they expected me to be ashamed of my joy but he was too high, right up under my breastbone so my breath kept coming too short and disturbing me so I couldn't really concentrate, I kept losing track of my mantra, and I got so restless I just had to do something so I asked Gran to get me some baby wool when she went out to the shops. I would have liked to choose it myself, just to get out of the flat because I felt like a prisoner, with nothing green and growing to look at except Gran's African violets and she wasn't dusting them any more so they were grey.

Gran didn't want to at first.

'That's a mistake,' she said. 'If you start knitting for it you're going to get attached.'

I had to beg her. 'Please Gran,' I said, 'please,' and I told her it was just for something to do with my hands because she'd like that. She was always on about the devil finding work for idle hands to do. 'And *you're* knitting for him,' I reminded her.

'That's different,' she said, and she actually looked guilty about it. 'It's not *my* baby and no poor little mite of a great-grandchild of mine is going to go into a foster home without a thread to put on its back.'

She got it for me in the end, wool and a pattern; most times Gran will do something if you really beg for it. She liked Mother and me to beg her for things and be grateful and beholden, and I showed her how grateful I was when she gave it to me, and I didn't say anything about the pattern being too difficult, but it was, terribly complicated with slipping and missing and through the back of the needle and loop the wool around, and for a while, until I more or less got the hang of it, Gran and I sat, saying nothing, just knitting for the baby that no one even wanted to talk about.

After a while it got so unnatural I just had to say something, so I said:

'You know, Gran, he can suck his thumb now? And he's even got hair and fingernails?'

Gran put her knitting down to get a better look at me.

'You'll not want to think about it,' she said. 'You'll want to keep your mind off it. Otherwise you'll get too attached.'

Gran just wouldn't believe that I was going to keep him, somehow, anyhow. And even if I weren't how could I stop myself from getting attached to him when he was attached to me, right inside me?

But I didn't say anything because I didn't want Gran to get more hassled than she already was. And I knew she was hassled. From where I was sitting I could see she was dropping more stitches than I was.

11

Mother

While I was working, for long periods at a stretch it would go out of my mind, just like amnesia, but little things would bring it all back again, someone in the office would say something about a baby, new or teething or ill, or a picture in the newspaper of a baby, a wedding or even just an advert for baby powder or gripe water and it would all come back with a little shock and I wondered how I could ever have forgotten, even for a second, but of course you can't be obsessed with the same thought day and night, that's madness, and God knows why, but I didn't actually go mad, I only felt I was, especially in the evenings when I got home and there she was and it felt like a heavy weight, an aching bruise, it weighed me down and made me feel bereft and resentful about having to feel like that.

I thought of everything I'd done for her, from the first minute I'd brought her home, how everything went wrong. When I took her nappy off her navel started to bleed and it wouldn't stop and she stiffened her legs and flailed her arms and started yelling and it seemed she didn't stop for three long months. And I got so frantic, checking for open pins and fleas and trying to give her her bottle which she was always sicking up and trying to bring up winds which always got stuck, giving her colic, and Gran repeating over and over, if she's fed, and her wind is brought up and she's warm and dry she'll sleep, only Girlie didn't and I was so exhausted I used to cry in the bathroom, into a bath towel because a hanky just didn't seem big enough to soak up all my misery and exhaustion, and Gran saying I was making a thing of it and letting it get on top of me but even Gran had to admit that she didn't know what was wrong, for the first time in her life she'd had to admit that, after

174

she'd been rocking the pram for about three hours, clucking and cooing away. In the end she was practically in the pram with Girlie. And then Frank said a terrible thing. Maybe he was also exhausted and exasperated and afraid, because he said:

'If you go on this way she's going to slip through your fingers.'

I don't think I ever forgave Frank for that. At least, I never forgot it. And now here she was and I couldn't help thinking maybe it would have been better if she *had* slipped through my fingers and it was such a terribly depressing thought that I felt like crying into a bath towel again. I even went to the bathroom and my eyes got misty but I couldn't cry. Everything was too tight inside me. I was too hopelessly screwed-up.

Then Phoebe, of all people, phoned. I listened to her breathing and I was so tight inside I couldn't say a word, I just stood there breathing myself, and we breathed at each other for quite a while until one of us, I can't remember who, put the phone down. And I thought now I *am* going to cry and I rushed to the bathroom and buried my face in the towel, but instead of crying I started laughing. I laughed and laughed, I actually wet myself, thinking, I should be crying, not laughing, I've got nothing to laugh about. But I couldn't help it, I just went on laughing, and I thought: it's happened, it's finally happened, it's taken this business to get me breathing like Phoebe, to get me to where Phoebe's got.

Gran

I had this feeling that everyone knew, the way they said: 'How are you?' making such a question of it, with their noses twitching, especially Esmé McKechnie and even Mrs Goedhals, although she usually minds her own business, just like hounds getting the scent of something. I had this feeling they knew and I hardly went out any more, except to get what we needed at the shops.

I knew it was just a feeling because nobody did know. Girlie never went out, like she'd promised, and I didn't feel too bad about that because I had moved my African violets so there was room for her in the sun around eleven o'clock every morning for her vitamin D and her poor little mite's bones, which meant the violets weren't getting any but people are more important, even from the time they're still unborn.

So no one knew but I couldn't get rid of this feeling of people talking behind my back. I could almost hear them. Have you heard about the Ferguson gel? Poor old Mrs Barker. And maybe it would have done me some good to get it off my chest and have a bit of sympathy from someone, but I didn't, so there was only Girlie to talk to until Iris came home and there we sat, day after day, knitting matinee jackets and little bootees that pulled at my heartstrings every time I finished a pair, because the poor little mite would have to go into a foster home, but I wasn't about to let it go empty-handed, no great-grandchild of mine was going to go anywhere empty-handed for the same reason that I was giving Girlie a balanced diet or as balanced as I could get on my housekeeping because no great-grandchild of mine who's got to go into a foster home is going to go unhealthy either.

So we were knitting a complete layette, Girlie and me, although we should have been making cloths and things for Girlie's bottom drawer, at her age, instead of matinee jackets for a fatherless baby, or at least I was making matinee jackets and Girlie was making ponchos because she isn't much of a knitter, like Iris, so I'd had to make Girlie's complete layette too.

I remembered it all, even that Iris wasn't much of a knitter, but at least that was a happier time, at least Iris was married even if it was only to Frank and I remember having had my doubts about him too.

Still there was nothing for it but to make the best of it, although ponchos didn't strike me as very suitable for a tiny baby, but Girlie couldn't knit anything else and at least he'd have more ponchos than any other baby ever had, even if he – or she – was having to go into a foster home, although Girlie's so sure it's a boy, which I didn't even want to think about, so I said to her:

'Maybe you should try some little bonnets, bonnets are quite easy,' but of course that only made me think about the poor little mite again and I had to stop thinking because I had just finished a little bootee with two little pom-poms on top and I thought my heart was going to break at the thought of not ever getting to see those little feet in them. I had to think about something else, so I said:

'Do you ever think about your father?' and I don't know why I said that, because I didn't want to think about him either, but it was out, and perhaps my thoughts were naturally running on fathers and husbands which I would have given my eye tooth for just then, for Girlie, if I had an eye tooth to give.

Girlie thought for a bit and then she said: 'I used to wonder why his mouth was always so dry.'

'I noticed that too,' I told her. 'You know mutton suet is wonderful for dry lips and chapped hands. You render it down and make it into cakes and use it every night, but your father wouldn't have none of it. He was a funny man.' And I nearly said, but at least he married your mother, but what was the use of going on and on about it? Only I couldn't seem to think of anything else to say at that time and that's not like me. Not that Girlie would have minded. She didn't seem to mind anything. She was sort of settled in, lumpy and gooey-eyed, like a bread pudding, I thought, with lots of jam on it.

Girlie

It took everything I had, all the discipline Vern had tried to teach me, to stop myself from getting as uptight as Mother and Gran were. It was bad enough when they were on at me all the time trying to blame someone, but it was worse when they sort of gave up on me and began to act like they'd blown their minds. Gran wasn't too bad, but the way Mother carried on, laughing into a towel like she was stoned really bugged me when I could have been quite happy, waiting for the baby and telling myself Vern wasn't really gone, he was striding the clouds and smiling in the wind because somehow, just then, the vibes were right, even there, shut up in that flat with only a thin slant of sun in the morning and no living thing except Gran and those dusty violets.

The vibes were right and my mind was free, it roamed, it really ranged, and I thought, I'm alive, it's life and I'm part of it, I'm carrying it, and I felt all humble because I'd been equipped and chosen to carry life and that humble feeling was happiness, because I'd done the right thing, respecting life, and I began to feel even happier and sorry for Vern because he'd never feel that way, and I thought poor Vern, poor men everywhere, they've lost out on this, they'll never know this.

Of course Vern knew what he knew, sitting out in the dark now, maybe, looking at the stars like he'd told me he loved to do, reciting their names like they were part of a mantra, stars he knew and could see without looking, the *Veil* in *Cygnus*, the *Rosette* in *Monceros* and the *Cluster* in *Berenice's Hair*.

Vern knew them all and he knew they weren't just white. The *Veil*, he said, was violet and blue, *Canes Venatici* was green and turquoise and the *Great Nebula* in *Andromeda* was lime green and gold.

He said he could get right up there amongst them, and I knew he was joking, but in a way I thought perhaps he could, to wheel and swirl with the *Nebula* maybe, and play with the gauze of the *Veil*.

Thinking about the stars made me think about God, suddenly, because He was supposed to be out there somewhere, deciding everything, like who was going to live and who was going to die and who was going to have a baby, like me. There was something tremendous in that, only I couldn't think what,

178

so I asked Mother. She'd had a baby.

'When you were expecting me,' I asked, 'did you think about God?'

'What God?' Mother said, getting all suspicious, like she thought I was having her on.

'God, you know,' I said, 'the God who makes babies.'

Mother began to laugh. 'Poor God,' she said. 'He gets blamed for everything.'

Gran looked like she was going to choke. 'Now just you give over, especially while you're in that condition,' she snapped. 'And remember your mother was legally married in the sight of God and man. If she did think about God, which I doubt, she had every right to!'

I left it at that because I didn't want the vibes to go bad again, and I thought, living out there among the stars, maybe God isn't as small-minded as Gran, because if she thought so highly of marriage, why had she been all for Mother getting a divorce? I knew they were wrong, both of them, but I didn't know who was right, except maybe God. And Vern.

Vern

I felt I could walk forever, foot down, roll on to the ball, heel up, the motion rhythmic, soporific, the distant convergence of the road my mark, getting smaller and smaller, narrowing to a pinpoint, always receding, and luring me on until I was nothing, concentrating so hard that I lost focus, the road, my feet and myself, everything except that pinpoint convergence, and that must have been it, the nearest I'd ever got to samadhi, but now a thought had begun to come with regularity, measuring my motion, spacing my stride: the turning of the seasons, the beach job if I wanted it again and Girlie who just might be looking for me there.

So now, with the grubs gone at last, I wanted to get back, to see if she would come, to see if maybe the grubs would stay away this time. A bright new corn-coloured car pulled up and the driver offered me a lift, calling out across the front seat in a dry scratchy voice. For a moment I hesitated. Cars weren't much better than the concrete and steel that always jangled my vibes, reactivating the grubs, but time was getting short if I wanted to make that job, and Girlie wouldn't know where else to look for me, if she was wanting to look for me.

I got in, thanked him and stowed my gear in the back where he told me to, and when we were moving he asked: 'Where are you heading?' Before I could answer he went on: 'Oh, I know, there and maybe back, you're the greatest, you children of the Universe, you're free, content with simply being ...

I had to take a good look at him, to see if he was a crazy. He had to be, I guessed, to offer me a lift in the first place, although he looked no more than half off, his skin a peculiar corn colour like his car, like teff in midwinter, but really sallow and sere, like he'd burst into flames the minute you put a match to him. His face was like the outcroppings of granite that knuckle the Lowveld, big-boned and hard-looking. He was the wearing a suit of shiny stuff that rustled when he moved, like flames licking through teff when rain is just a memory and everything is powdery and dry.

'I envy you, you know,' he said. 'You don't need to verbalise. What

is, is meaning enough, isn't it? Oh, the Woodstock spirit, make love not war, no need for absolutes, for trying to make some sense of the senseless ...'

He'd been staring straight ahead, hands lightly on the wheel, talking in a monotone as if to himself, but now he turned suddenly to look at me, eyes granite-grey and flint-hard in his heavy-boned face.

'What I'd like to know is, is all this an act of choice, existentialist choice, even, or is it instinctive? Is a lack of convictions what you're convinced of? Or is that cerebrating too much?'

That was where I began to tune out like I always do when someone asks me a question directly, especially a question about convictions, but he droned on, eyes fixed unwaveringly on the road ahead, about the world being in chaos and therefore everything was irrelevant anyway, all effort and especially creative effort, which was why I was rebelling, wasn't it? And he looked at me so long and hard that I had to say something.

'I don't know,' I said. 'Am I rebelling?'

He laughed a dry, hard laugh and put his left hand out to squeeze my knee.

'Forget it. I'm with you,' and he began to stroke my thigh, rather roughly. 'Although, like Ionesco, I'm not sure that everything is unsayable in words, except perhaps the living truth, whatever that may be ...'

He was quiet for a time, really working on my thigh, like a physio-therapist, and I wondered if I could say, drop me here, this is as far as I go, right in the middle of the bush, but he'd know I was really saying no way, and he scared me. He was a crazy all right.

He began to talk again, the tiny muscle at the side of his mouth bouncing like a pebble as he quarried his words:

'I've got a pad in the city, rather plush, I'm afraid, but you're welcome. Stay as long as you like, come and go as you like, even ...'

I was already squashed up against the door, trying to get away from that hard exploring hand that was beginning to leave a tingle under my skin so like the grubs that I was losing my cool, my breathing too shallow and quick as panic began to surge.

'I've got to make the coast,' I told him, 'for the season, my girl's *there waiting for me.'*

He stopped right there with a squeal of brakes and actually ground his big yellow teeth at me.

'I'm not going that far,' he said, 'and anyway I was having you on, because what I really think of you, the lot of you, hiking around, living like parasites, makes me puke ...'

He needn't have punched me out of the car like he did, cracking my head against the door, because I couldn't wait to get away from him and his relentlessness that was like a hand squeezing my throat, so much I even forgot my gear, still stowed in the back, until he'd roared off, until the car was no more than a pale sunspot flaming off a distant curve of the road.

I stood there for a while, telling myself to hang loose, to just breathe, it was like before, only a bit slower now, with no gear, but like before ...

I moved on slowly, trying to concentrate, on to the ball, left foot rising, only I was all jangled now, my motion so confused that my right foot turned in and I tripped, catching split-second impressions as I went down, a hawk, a telegraph pole, a locust bending a blade of grass on the side of the road and a smear of blood and fur on the tarmac, all that was left of a dassie and I thought wow! hearing the great rush of sound getting louder by the second as a car bore down on me. I told myself, move, man, up! or you're going to be that, a commingling of blood and bone and squashed gut, spread out thin, papering the highway ... but the roar was on me, ruffling my hair, and I heard the driver's curse funnelling out behind him before everything burst open, whining deadly like shrapnel in my head.

For a moment or two I scrambled after consciousness, after the shards and splinters of thought that cohered into bullets of shock ricocheting around inside me: I'm hit, like that dassie, how will she know ...

I tried to beat out the fire of fear and pain that was beginning to lick at me, but everything was losing shape, becoming fluid, I could feel my body, my fingers swelling, becoming fluid, growing fat, thin, wavering, until I couldn't bring my mind to bear any longer, as it grew fluid too, rippling right away from me ...

Part Three

1

Gran

I had to talk to Girlie again. She'd had a good while to think now and if her predicament hadn't sunk in the last time I tried, it'd had time to sink in now. With her nearly ready to pop, she'd realise it wasn't a laughing matter any more, and she'd got to think about it, it was getting too late in the day to be pussyfooting around, we couldn't go on sitting like two bees in a honeycomb, pretending there was nothing unusual and no real plans to be made for the future. So I went along to her where she was lying down, and I thought, at least she can't sit with her toes curling up under her any more, and I gave her some kindness and love in my smile because that's what a Gran is for and I asked her just what advice that mother of hers had been giving her, if any.

'Advice?' she asks me like she's never heard the word before and I couldn't help thinking, she needs a good hard slap she does and not too late for it neither, although it would have done more good given in time. Spare the rod and spoil the child, there's always a grain of truth in these old sayings if you've only got the patience to look for it.

'Yes, advice!' I said to her. 'She's your mother isn't she, so she must have given you some advice?' because I suspected that Iris must be encouraging Girlie behind my back in her obstinacy or she would never think of trying to rear a fatherless child right under the noses of respectable people, and people like Esmé McKechnie.

'Advice about what?' she asks, as if that disgrace of a stomach didn't belong to her.

'About your predicament,' I said. 'I do suppose you realise by now that you're in a predicament? And what I want to know is what she advised you to do because there isn't so much time left, you've got to make up your mind now and lay your plans and it's that that I'm talking about!' Time was getting short and I would give it to her all right if it was the truth she was wanting. Never held my tongue for anyone when I was roused, least of all for her who's my own granddaughter, never been afraid to tell anyone the truth, say just what I think, and they can put that on my tombstone one day.

'Oh, she said I must have him adopted,' Girlie said then, quick, like she was wanting to answer and get rid of me, so I stood for a little, saying nothing, to show her I'll come and I'll go and I'll talk and I'll shut up all in my own good time and when I feel like it, not a moment before and not a moment after, thanks very much, especially when time was getting so short.

'All right then,' I said. 'She's quite right. That's what you have to do before people like Esmé McKechnie find out. There's no question about it.' And I smiled at her again, to show that it was all settled and over, but she didn't smile back, oh no, never even said come in, Gran, sit down, it's nice of you to be so concerned on my behalf, oh no, she just lies there, all obstinate like, with that do-what-you-damn-well-please-and-good-luck-to-you sort of look that she's got on her face lately that's rather pudgy now, as I notice, sort of swollen up around the cheeks like a squirrel with a mouthful of nuts.

'What are you now?' I asked her. 'Just about due?' She looked ready to pop to me, swollen right up to the eyeballs like that.

'You've been putting on a mite too much weight,' I told her, to take her mind off the other business, because I'm not saying it's easy, giving up a baby you've carried for nine months and laboured to bring into the world. She had all my sympathy, but there was no other way out of it that I could see and she couldn't rightly expect to get away with it, but it wasn't for me to add to her burden, so I advised her, with all the kindness in the world:

'You'll need to be careful now, at the last like this, the more weight, the bigger the baby, the harder the birth, you cut down a bit on the fats and the starches,' I told her, but she just lay there, not an expression on her face, just like a mummy, I thought, and a mummy-to-be at that, which struck me as rather funny and I had to laugh out loud because I always did have a turn of phrase, but she looked at me like she thought I'd gone mad but of course she didn't know what the joke was and she hadn't got anything to laugh about herself, in her predicament, so I fell to feeling sorry for her again, now that I'd got her to do the right thing, and thinking of the pain and the suffering she still had to go through, I said:

'I'll make you some cocoa, Girlie, a little bit more weight is going to be neither here nor there now and I'll make it with milk which is a touch extravagant, but what's life all about if you can't break out a little now and then, eh?'

'Gran,' she said to me, 'I don't want any cocoa.'

'Of course you want cocoa,' I told her.

'And I'm not giving up my baby.'

It was the way she said it that made me feel feeble all of a sudden so that I had to sit down on Iris's bed.

'I'm sorry,' she said, and I could see she really was, but for *me* as though I was senile or stupid and she had to humour me. I stared at her and if I didn't *know* she was Iris's child I would have thought no, she doesn't belong to us, she can't be a part of us.

She got up then, even clumsier than usual and said: 'I'll make *you* some cocoa, Gran,' and she was gone into the kitchen before I could say another word, not that there was another word to say, because for the first time in my whole life I couldn't think of another word. I didn't understand her, she might be Iris's daughter, but I just couldn't see how she could have got to be a granddaughter of mine.

Girlie

I was so big and hot and uncomfortable, sweating all the time and short of breath. My back ached and my legs throbbed and

I felt I just couldn't wait any longer. Mother and Gran were always on about shows and the water breaking and I thought they'd be interested so I said to them:

'Did you know that the weight of that fertilised egg has been increased five thousand million times?'

But that didn't grab them at all, they just said it wasn't necessary to talk about things like that.

'Like what?' I asked, because you never know with them.

'Fertilised eggs,' Mother said.

'Any sort of eggs,' Gran said, 'at a time like this.'

And then about an hour later I finally got that show they were talking about and I couldn't believe it. It's funny, but after waiting nine months, when the time came, I just couldn't believe it. I checked over the things in my suitcase, to waste time before going to tell Mother and Gran, because I had the feeling that they still didn't believe it was all really happening. It was too much for them, and I was scared that when I went in and said:

'I think the baby's coming,' there would be the same scandalised shock and hassling and I'd have to go through the whole bit again.

But when I was afraid to wait any longer I did go in and I said:

'I'll be getting along now, I think. I'll just take the bus.'

Gran said: 'Here, what's all this about?'

'I'll be off now,' I told her.

'Off?' Mother said.

'Off?' Gran said. 'Don't be silly, you're on your last legs, how can you be off anywhere?'

'No,' I said, 'I don't mean that, I mean, that's just it. If I don't go now I won't even be on my last legs,' trying to make a joke of it.

But you couldn't make a joke with them, they were too uptight about everything. They jumped up, both of them and started to yell and flap around me.

'You don't mean ... ?' Mother yelled, and Gran yelled: 'Dear merciful …'

'Look, it's all right,' I told them. 'I've got time. I'll just take the bus.'

'The bus!' they both shrieked. And Gran said: 'Do you want everybody to *know*?'

Mother staggered blindly to the phone and fumbled for the receiver.

'I'm ringing for a taxi,' she said. 'You're sure? You've got a show? I hope to God the waters don't break. We're getting a taxi. You're not going to have any baby that's a grandchild of mine on a bus.' She went on fumbling with the phone until Gran took it from her.

'You'll be wanting to get a hold of yourself, Iris,' she said to Mother. 'It's bad enough for the poor gel that hasn't got a husband to stand by her at the eleventh hour like this. Have you thought of that?'

'Thought of it?' Mother screams, taking the phone off Gran. 'What else have I thought about? Where in God's name is the number?'

I looked up the number and phoned myself while Mother and Gran flapped around doing nothing that I could see. Then Mother screamed again:

'Dr Shaw! We've got to phone Dr Shaw!'

I did that as well and then I said goodbye and tried to kiss them both.

'Goodbye?' Mother screamed. 'What do you mean goodbye? I'm not going to let you go into this alone without a husband,' and then they both dashed around getting their coats and handbags and closing all the windows. Then they tried to disguise me by wrapping a scarf around my head and sticking sunglasses on my nose so I couldn't see a thing because it was dark outside. I could have done without all that and I'd rather have gone alone but it was no use arguing with them. By then they were both beyond reason.

In the taxi they held my hands tightly, one on each side. 'You'll not want to worry,' Gran told me. 'You're not the first gel who's ever had a baby. Just remember that.'

'Dr Shaw is very experienced,' Mother said. 'If anything does go wrong he's going to call in a specialist straight away, I told him to, so there's no need to worry.'

'Now that's a silly thing to say, Iris,' Gran said. 'If anything goes wrong. What are you trying to do, scare the poor gel out of her wits? It's bad enough just having a baby even if *nothing* goes wrong!'

'Now don't you worry,' Mother said to me. 'We'll be there, Gran and I, we won't leave you.'

'Needs to be horsewhipped, that young man,' Gran said. 'Getting a gel in a condition like this and then leaving her when she needs a husband.'

'Don't go on and on about it,' Mother said. 'It's bad enough as it is. You're just making her nervous. She doesn't want to get her muscles all tightened up.'

I sort of shrank between them and closed my eyes. That was a mistake because Mother began to chafe the skin off my wrists and Gran scrabbled for her eau de cologne and fanned my face with her hankie.

'I'm all right,' I told them. 'I'm not worried. I'm not nervous. I'm all right. It's a natural thing.'

'There isn't anything natural about it without a husband,' Gran said.

'Shhhhh,' Mother said, pointing frantically at the taxi driver's neck. 'It's a pity ... uh ... Ron is away at a time like this,' she said very loudly, 'every father should be around at a time like this. But business ...'

'Eh?' Gran said. 'Who's Ron?'

'Shhhhh,' Mother hissed at her. 'You know who Ron is. Girlie's *husband*!' and she jabbed at the taxi driver's neck.

Gran leaned over me, very worried, to look into Mother's face. 'Iris?' she asked. 'Are you feeling all right?'

We turned in at the hospital and Gran scrambled out, still looking at Mother and asking: 'Here. What's all this about a husband?'

Mother paid the driver, telling him about three times about my husband Ron who was away on business, so unfortunate. Then she made me put on Gran's wedding ring which was too big for me.

'Just tell all the nurses that your husband Ron is away on business,' she said, while Gran kept plucking at her sleeve and asking:

'If you know his name why don't you get him back here to make an honest woman of her? It's still not too late, you knew. There'll be a few hours to go yet.'

'I told you I don't know his name,' Mother said.

'But why then ...' Gran kept asking, and they were still at it when Dr Shaw came and told them to go home, he'd phone them as soon as there was any news.

I was very grateful to him for that. He told me everything was going to be fine, there was nothing to worry about. But I wasn't worried. To help with the pains I fixed my attention and repeated a mantra over and over which worked quite well until I started to throw up, heaving so violently that I thought the baby was going to come out of my mouth.

It didn't, of course, it came, finally, in the usual way, and when it was all over I began to cry, not with grief or joy, but a profound emptiness.

'That's all right, get it off your chest,' Dr Shaw told me. 'A touch of post-partum blues, that's all.'

I didn't care what it was called, I went on crying, like I should have cried and couldn't when Vern was leaving, when I was trying to play it so cool I just dried up, my hands and my tongue and my lips, all dry, like my father's, and I thought it would have taken a ton of mutton suet or whatever it was rendered down to get rid of that dryness that was so terrible I couldn't even speak.

He'd said next summer, which was now, but only 'maybe'. Still, I thought, just as soon as I could I'd go down there and maybe I'd find him, sitting quiet and dark like an Indian, with the sand sifting over him.

And if he wasn't there I wanted him to be where there was no sweat, where the ericas didn't give out on to dry ground and a camp where people were put out like chickens to scratch for life, where cripples didn't march and the roads weren't tarred with fur and blood; in Kathmandu, perhaps, bathing in a well and rapping with the monks, where the vibes were so good he could get right up there amongst the stars without any effort; to stroke the *Horsehead* in *Orion* or juggle with the *Rings* in *Lyra* ...

Mother

I couldn't believe it, Girlie having a baby went through my head clackety clacking like a train. I couldn't believe it. She was only just a baby herself. The waiting was getting on my nerves, I had to talk, so I said to Gran:

'Do you remember how Girlie never slept, when she was a baby?'

'You never brought up her wind properly,' Gran said.

'She had colic,' I told her.

'Nonsense,' Gran said. 'There isn't any such thing.'

'She had thrush too,' I said.

'You didn't wash your nipples properly,' Gran said.

'She was on the bottle,' I reminded her.

'That's why then,' Gran said. She always gets argumentative when she's tense. 'You never got thrush. None of my friends' babies ever got thrush. We washed our nipples and put little lace hankies over the breast when we fed our babies.'

'And then when she *did* occasionally sleep,' I said, 'you used to pick her up and wake her again.'

'Nonsense,' Gran said. 'They never wake up when they're small. It's the only time you can fondle them without spoiling them, when they're asleep.'

I didn't really feel like arguing just then but I had to talk or

I might have started screaming, so I asked her:

'And what about the germs on the hankie?'

'You boil the hankie,' she said.

'And by the time you get the hankie to the breast it's full of germs again.'

'We didn't have so many germs in my day,' Gran said. 'And if we did we didn't know about them. That makes all the difference.'

When the phone finally rang Gran got to it the same time as I did, but I answered it and I had to try three or four times before I managed to tell her:

'It's a girl!'

It took Gran a few seconds to catch her breath and when *she* could talk again she said:

'Knew it all along. I could see from the way it was lying. I said it would be a gel all along, didn't I?'

'Yes Gran,' I said, and then I started to cry.

Gran

I was still thinking it can't be happening, because it shouldn't be happening, that's what, but I was fine until I started having trouble with my breathing and I knew I was in for a stroke after all, after all these years.

'We'll take a taxi,' Iris was blubbering.

'What for?' I asked, because I was feeling really limp and breathless.

'To see Girlie of course,' she howled, 'and the baby. Girlie has got no one else to go and see her. She hasn't even got a husband to go and see her.'

'Well don't keep harping on it,' I told her. 'It's not nice.'

'On what?' Iris asks and she can hardly ring for the taxi, the way she's wailing.

'On her having no husband,' I said. 'We all know that, the

more's the pity. We'll go and see Girlie but,' and I began to get all breathless again, 'do you think we should see the baby? Maybe that's a mistake, maybe we'll get too attached to it and then ...'

Iris's face crumpled up even further and she sat down. 'My grandchild,' she cried.

I had to feel sorry for her, and my strength was beginning to come back. 'All right,' I said, 'and my great-grandchild, so will it help us to sit blubbering about it? What's done is done. Nothing you can do about it.' I'm a great believer in philosophy and I think that carried me through although I could feel I was on the verge of having a stroke.

When we got to the hospital with Iris still howling away, Girlie looked tired but sort of full of herself, just as if it didn't matter that she didn't have a husband.

'Now I've got to think of a name,' she said and that set Iris off blubbering again.

'I don't think you can name it when it's going up for adoption,' I told her, because it's best to get these things straight, right at the beginning. 'I know there's these actresses having babies right out of holy wedlock and keeping them but this isn't Hollywood.'

'I thought of Gabrielle,' Girlie said. She was developing the knack of ignoring me, just like Iris did sometimes. 'Because she looks like an angel.'

'Gabrielle!' I said. 'That's a name for an actress. Too flashy by half.'

'Maybe Iris,' Girlie said. 'I did think of Iris.'

'Oh Girlie,' Iris shrieks, going at it like a waterfall.

'If,' I told Girlie, 'if you had the sense to get yourself married, and if you could keep the baby and if you could name her, there's always Beulah.'

'Beulah?' Girlie asks, looking at me for the first time, or at anyone for that matter, because she'd got her eyes fixed on the ceiling as though she was having a private preview of Heaven.

'It means joy,' I told her. 'My late mother, that is your great-grandmother named me Beulah, for joy. But then she was married of course.'

'Beulah for joy,' Girlie, says and I could see that it had struck her. "Sweet Joy I call thee".'

Well, I'd always thought it a good name, only I had to remind her:

'It wouldn't do in this case, though, because where's the joy?'

I didn't feel any joy, not much, and neither did Iris, the way she was snivelling, but of course Girlie was quite shameless and it was right there, all over her face. It was so embarrassing in the circumstances that I was almost glad when the sister called us to look at the baby, which I wasn't really in favour of in case we got too attached, but the way Iris stampeded out I had to go along just to see she didn't do something silly, and it's hard, not to be able to have just one little peek at your own first great-granddaughter.

And I had to take a strong hold of myself when I did see her because, poor fatherless little mite that she was, she looked just like me. A good head of hair, on the curly side, and blue eyes that I could see were going to stay blue.

'Well, we'll have to make the best of it,' I told Iris who couldn't have seen a thing through that waterfall she was weeping, and I thought, if only that silly gel had had the good sense to get married like everyone else we could all have been in the newspapers and I could just see Esmé McKechnie's face.

Four generations, all gels. The papers love pictures like that.